NELLIE OLESON MEETS LAURA INGALLS

LITTLE HOUSE · BIG ADVENTURE

by LAURA INGALLS WILDER

LITTLE HOUSE IN THE BIG WOODS

FARMER BOY

LITTLE HOUSE ON THE PRAIRIE

ON THE BANKS OF PLUM CREEK

BY THE SHORES OF SILVER LAKE

THE LONG WINTER

LITTLE TOWN ON THE PRAIRIE

THESE HAPPY GOLDEN YEARS

THE FIRST FOUR YEARS

by CYNTHIA RYLANT

OLD TOWN IN THE GREEN GROVES
*Laura Ingalls Wilder's
Lost Little House Years*

NELLIE OLESON MEETS
LAURA INGALLS

by HEATHER WILLIAMS

HarperCollins*Publishers*

HarperCollins®, ®, and Little House® are
trademarks of HarperCollins Publishers.

Library of Congress Cataloging-in-Publication Data is available.
Williams, Heather, date
   Nellie Oleson meets Laura Ingalls / Heather Williams.— 1st ed.
      p.   cm.
   Summary: Wealthy, spoiled Nellie Oleson is only happy when she is the
center of attention, and so she feels angry and left out when Laura Ingalls,
a poor country girl, moves to Walnut Grove and is embraced by Nellie's
friends and schoolteacher.
   ISBN 978-0-06-124248-9 (trade bdg.)
   ISBN 978-0-06-124249-6 (lib. bdg.)
   [1. Frontier and pioneer life—Great Plains—Fiction. 2. Schools—
Fiction. 3. Behavior—Fiction. 4. Wilder, Laura Ingalls, 1867–1957—
Fiction. 5. Great Plains—Fiction.] 1. Title.
PZ7.W662Nel 2007   2007010907
[Fic]—dc22   CIP
                                                               AC

Typography by Christopher Stengel
1 2 3 4 5 6 7 8 9 10
❖
First Edition

CONTENTS

STRANGER IN THE STORE

Nellie Oleson did not like the prairie.

She did not like the dust. She did not like the big open sky. She did not like how there was nothing to see in any direction for miles and miles and miles. She did not like the musky, hot, itchy smell of horses tied up along Main Street, or the wind that whistled all night and blew dirt in her face all day.

She hated the long, boring afternoons when she was cooped up in her father's store. She hated the flies that came in through the open windows and the men in raggedy clothes who came in through the open door.

She couldn't go outside to play. She had to keep her skin pale and ladylike. But she didn't want to go out anyway. It was always too hot or too cold. In the summer there were too many bugs, and in the winter her fingers and toes were always frozen.

Every morning when Nellie woke up, she lay in bed for as long as she could, wishing and wishing that her father would take them back to New York. They had come west when she was only a little girl, so she could not remember their home back east very well. But she knew it had to be better than Walnut Grove.

When she was very small, her family had taken a trip to New York City. Nellie was sure it was the biggest, most beautiful city in the world.

New York had buildings that reached so far up into the sky, she imagined clouds must bump into them all the time. She could remember the streets full of well-dressed people walking and talking. Everywhere she heard the clop-clopping sound of hooves on stone as horse-drawn carriages went by.

Most of all she remembered big store windows made of clear, shiny glass. She had pulled away from her mother's hand to press her nose against their smooth, clean surfaces. Beyond, she could see a world of silk dresses and gloves and velvet hats and polished shoes. Mrs. Oleson was very angry when she finally found Nellie, but Nellie didn't care.

She knew New York was the place for her. There was something to see wherever you looked. Not like on the prairie, where she had nothing to do all day long. At least, nothing she wanted to do.

Every night Nellie sat in front of the great looking-glass in the bedroom as her mother brushed her long golden hair and wrapped it in curl-papers. Nellie would look into her own blue eyes and dream about being a grown lady. When she was old enough, she could go back to New York and be a real city girl. She would wear fine dresses and hoopskirts and delicate slippers. Elegant men would ask her to dance. New York was a good place to be beautiful, and Nellie Oleson was very beautiful.

"Take care of your looks, Nellie," Mrs. Oleson always said. "A rich man will marry you someday if you are pretty. That's the most important thing you have to remember."

Nellie didn't see how she was ever going to meet a rich man out here on the prairie, especially one she would want to marry. She had not met a single person in Walnut Grove who she thought was good enough to even speak to the Oleson family.

She knew her mother felt the same way, because Mrs. Oleson had a way of sniffing when she disapproved of someone. Nearly everyone who came into the store got Mrs. Oleson's *sniff-sniff* of disapproval once they were gone.

One spring morning when Nellie was seven years old, she was in her father's store, dusting. This was a job she hated. The dust tickled her nose, and it made her hands feel dry and rough. But every Saturday her father called her into the store, handed her a damp rag, and pointed her to the shelves behind the counter. Her little brother, Willie, had only one chore, sweeping the front steps, because he was younger than her and a boy. Nellie did not think that was fair.

The store was big, but it was so crowded with merchandise that it looked much smaller. In the front it was lit by the sun coming through the two windows and the open door. But toward the back it could be dim and hard to see, especially on dark winter days.

Along one side of the store was a long board counter. Behind it the wall was covered in shelves that reached nearly to the ceiling. Each shelf was crammed with pans and pots and pieces of stovepipe and hinges and door knobs and tin cups and pails and bolts of cloth in bright reds and soft browns and cornsilk yellows. It was Nellie's task to dust everything she could reach until it shone. Then her mother would dust everything else that she couldn't reach.

Mr. Oleson said it was important for everything to be clean so that it gleamed in the lamplight. Nobody wanted to buy dusty pots, he told Nellie. And dust blew in off the street all day long as people came in and out. It made

Nellie dislike the shop's customers more and more, as she watched the store get dirtier with every person who tromped in. She knew she would have to help her mother clean it later. At least she did not have to do any chores that would tan her skin or give her hands calluses.

The only good thing about this chore was that her father usually did not watch her while she did it. He always faced forward over the counter, selling or joking with customers.

Along the opposite wall were all the sharp and dangerous things: knives, saws, axes, wires, nails, hoes, hatchets, and farming tools. Nellie and Willie were not allowed to touch anything on that side of the store, because they might hurt themselves. Willie would sometimes sneak over and pick up hatchets or hammers when no one was looking, but Nellie was just pleased that she did not have to dust them. And while her father was across the store cleaning plows, Nellie could crouch down behind the counter and dust as slowly and as badly as she wanted.

Nellie knew she was supposed to pick up each pot and wipe her rag over the whole inside and outside. But she also knew that the customers could see only the front of a pot from the counter. So she only dusted that part. She couldn't see what difference it made. Her father never had any trouble selling them. And she had never been scolded for it, so it could not be very important.

Nellie heard the bell jingle as the screen door opened and shut. She scrunched herself farther down behind the counter. She hated to be seen when she was doing chores for her father. She wanted the other children in town to think that she never had to do any work, because she was perfect, pretty, rich little Nellie Oleson.

Slow footsteps came along the boards, and Nellie heard a strange voice say: "Are you William Oleson?"

Her father answered, "I am."

"Charles Ingalls," the man said in a friendly way. Nellie did not recognize the name or the man's voice. He must be new in town. She guessed that he was shaking hands with her father. "A fine town you have here. My family has just arrived. We've traded for the Hanson claim. I understand this is the place to come for supplies."

"Anything and everything," Mr. Oleson said. Nellie felt proud. There were two other general stores in town, Mr. Beadle's and Mr. Fitch's. But her father's store was the best.

They had borrowed money from relatives when they came west so that they could stock the store with lots and lots of everything. Mr. Oleson said it was important to start out right. He said they could pay the money back later, but they must be the best-stocked store right from the start.

And it was working. Her father was one of the richest men in town. Nellie and Willie were allowed to take anything they wanted from the store. Her ma said, "William, can we really afford it?" and her pa answered, "Of course, Margaret. We're shopkeepers, not farmers! There's plenty of inventory. The children can have whatever they want." So Nellie always had the prettiest boughten dresses, first pick of the colorful ribbons, and all the candy she could eat.

"I'm looking for a tin stove and two pieces

of stovepipe," Mr. Ingalls said.

That meant they would come behind the counter. Nellie did not want this strange man to see her. She crept along fast as a mouse to the back of the store.

But at the end of the counter she ran into a pair of boots. The first thing she saw was a hole in one toe. And then she looked up, up, up until she saw the man's twinkling blue eyes looking down at her.

He was tall, with a full brown beard. Apart from the hole in his boots, his clothes were clean and well mended. He did not smell of tobacco or spirits like some of the other men who came into the store.

"Why, hello," Mr. Ingalls said. His voice was solemn, but his eyes looked as if he was laughing at her. Nellie decided right away that she did not like him. He did not say, "What a pretty little girl," the way most people did when they saw her. Nellie scrambled to her feet, feeling her face turn red.

"This is my daughter, Nellie," Mr. Oleson said. He reached up to a high shelf for the stovepipe. "Nellie, say hello to Mr. Ingalls."

Nellie did not want to say hello. She turned up her nose, just as she had seen her mother do. She went *sniff-sniff* to show that she did not think much of this hairy farmer. And then she stomped off to the back of the store with her head held high and her curls bouncing.

Mr. Ingalls looked surprised that she had disobeyed her father. But he did not say anything, and neither did Mr. Oleson. Nellie knew that her father would not scold her. He did not care how she behaved. He only cared about the store making money.

Nellie flounced through the back door of the store into the Olesons' parlor. Her mother was sitting at the table doing accounts. She did not look up as Nellie came in. Nellie stomped her feet as hard as she could on the rug. But Mrs. Oleson kept adding and doing sums. So Nellie went into the bedroom and threw herself on the bed to sulk.

After a while she got bored with nobody noticing her. She got up and took her china doll out of the bottom drawer where she kept her toys. She had gotten the doll for Christmas last year, and she loved her. The doll had wavy black china hair and tiny china hands and beautiful china feet in black shoes. Nellie had to be careful with her or she would break. And she had to be extra careful not to let Willie touch her.

Her brother, Willie, was trouble. He was only six, but he was already mean as a snake. He broke things just for fun, and he was always making mischief. This was good because he got in much more trouble than Nellie. Mr. and Mrs. Oleson thought Nellie was a perfect angel next to Willie. But it was bad because sometimes the things he broke were Nellie's. Nellie did not like Willie very much.

She could not let Willie know that she loved her china doll, or he might break her just to be spiteful. So Nellie played with her only when he was outside.

Nellie lifted the doll carefully out of the drawer. She touched her smooth black hair and red cheeks.

"Hello, Laura," she whispered. That was her

doll's name. Nellie's favorite aunt back east was named Laura. Nellie thought the doll was as beautiful and elegant as her aunt Laura.

She walked the doll across the bedspread. One day she would be elegant, too. She would marry someone rich and she would never have to do chores. She could be as delicate as a china doll. And she would not have to live on the prairie ever again.

SCHOOL DAY

On Monday morning Mrs. Oleson called Nellie to get ready for school.

Nellie pulled the sheet over her head. If she did not wake up, maybe her mother would come and make her get up.

She heard the clinking of china dishes in the parlor. She smelled corn bread fresh from baking in the iron cookstove. She heard Willie kick the table legs and yell that he wanted more molasses. She heard her father push his chair back and go into the store.

Nobody came to make sure she woke up.

Finally Nellie got out of bed in a huff. She had to hurry into her pink dress with lace on the cuffs and the trim. She had to wash her face and hands quickly from the big china pitcher of water her mother had left on the dresser. Then she had to hunt all over the bedroom for her shoes, which she had kicked away as she'd undressed the night before. At last she found them under the bed, where it was dusty. So she had to wash her hands again.

By the time she came into the parlor, she was very angry.

Mrs. Oleson did not notice that Nellie was deliberately late. She did not notice that Nellie was mad. Mrs. Oleson turned Nellie around and did up her buttons. She unwrapped the curl-papers from Nellie's hair and tied two big pink bows on top of her head. Nellie felt like a china doll, only when her mother finished, she gave Nellie a little push instead of patting her on the head.

"Off you go," Mrs. Oleson said. She gave Nellie her slate and slate pencil and books. "You can eat a piece of corn bread as you walk."

"I'm not hungry," Nellie said, scowling.

"Come *on*, Nellie," said Willie. He was standing by the door to the store, jumping from one foot to the other.

"All right," said Mrs. Oleson. "Then I will see you for dinner."

As they went through the store, Willie grabbed some candy from a tall wooden pail in front of the counter. Mr. Oleson was talking to a customer and did not say anything to them.

Outside, the prairie wind was blowing dust along Main Street. Nellie scrunched her eyes nearly shut to keep the dust out. Across the street, Mr. Fitch was sweeping the steps of his store. He waved to them. Willie waved back, but Nellie did not. She didn't like it when people bought supplies at Mr. Fitch's store instead of from her pa.

The air smelled like smoke from all the stovepipes of the houses in town. The sky up above was clear blue, with long streaks of white clouds like milk spilled across a tablecloth. It was going to be another hot day.

"Nellie!" a voice called behind her. "Nellie Oleson!"

Nellie looked back. Christy Kennedy and her sister Cassie were running to catch up with them. Nellie thought about pretending that she hadn't heard them. But Christy was nice and sometimes funny, even if she had too many freckles and wore shoes only in winter.

Nellie stopped outside the lumber-yard to wait while Willie kept going. Small curls of wood shavings danced across the road. They bounced just like her curls. Beneath her shoes there were scatterings of sawdust, and the air smelled like newly cut wood.

Christy Kennedy had bright red hair. She wore it in two braids pulled so tight, Nellie sometimes wanted to tug on them to see if they would snap off. She had two older sisters, one older brother, and a little brother named Sandy, who was Willie's friend.

Nellie was very glad she did not have any older sisters. Christy often wore dresses and coats that were handed down from Cassie, with patches on the elbows or let-down hems.

Nellie liked having new clothes that were all her own.

"Hello, Nellie," Christy said as she caught up. Her face was flushed, and her sunbonnet was swinging down her back.

"You should wear your sunbonnet," Nellie said. No wonder Christy had so many freckles. "Hasn't your mother told you how to take care of your looks?"

"Looks!" Christy said. "I'm only seven."

Nellie thought that was a silly thing to say, but before she could say so, Christy grabbed her hand.

"Come on, we'd better hurry," she said. "We don't want to be late!"

That made Nellie mad all over again. She wouldn't have been late if she hadn't stopped to wait for Christy!

She pulled her hand back. "I'm not going to *run*."

"All right," Christy said with a shrug, and ran on ahead.

Nellie followed her slowly down the long path to the new schoolhouse. Nellie had watched the men of the town building it last summer.

Everyone else was already inside. Miss Eva Beadle, the teacher, was standing at the door holding the school bell. Miss Beadle was very pretty in a grown-up way. She wore her brown hair in bangs with thick braids pinned up behind her head. Nellie thought she might wear her hair like that when she was older. But she would not be a schoolteacher. Not her! Only poor girls had to be teachers.

"Good morning, Nellie," Teacher said. "I'm sure you will try not to keep everyone waiting tomorrow."

Nellie turned up her nose and marched past her into the schoolhouse. She wasn't sure what she thought of Miss Beadle. At first she'd been determined not to like her. Miss Beadle was Mr. Beadle's sister, and Mr. Beadle owned one of the other general stores in town, so Nellie intended not to like either of them. Furthermore, Teacher never treated Nellie as if she was special. She didn't seem to know that Nellie was rich, or notice that she was pretty. She treated her exactly like all her other pupils, even the poorest ones.

But sometimes Teacher would smile at Nellie and tell her she'd done something well. And then Nellie felt a strange little glow inside, like a spark in her chest. When Teacher smiled at her, it made Nellie want to smile back. So sometimes she thought maybe she did like Miss Beadle. But most of the time she was sure she did not.

Because she was late, Nellie had to sit at the end of a bench, beside Christy and behind Maud. That put her next to one of the schoolhouse's glass windows. Teacher left the windows and door open when the weather was nice. This was another reason Nellie didn't like her. The wind came sailing through the windows and mussed Nellie's hair. The dust blew in and made her sneeze. Worst of all, there were always flies and other bugs flying in and out, buzzing and biting and crawling around.

Today Nellie did not feel like studying her letters. She opened her speller and propped her slate against it, but she was too mad to practice reading. She couldn't remember why she was mad. She just knew she was having a bad day.

Time crawled by, slow as molasses. Nellie stared out the window and swung her feet. When she got bored with looking at the prairie, she stared at the back of Maud's head. Teacher was working on arithmetic with Willie and the younger children. Christy had one end of a braid stuck in her mouth and was studying her reader.

Something buzzed against the top of the window and then butted its way down the glass until it hit the air and came in. Nellie watched it idly. As it came closer, she saw that it was a hornet. Its wings flew almost too fast to see. The yellow and black stripes on its body were bright and shiny in the sunshine. It landed on the back of the bench in front of Nellie.

She watched it crawl slowly along the wooden board toward Maud. Maud was Nellie's age. She had short, straight yellow hair tied back with a red ribbon.

Nellie leaned over to Christy and whispered, "I bet you that hornet stings Maud."

Teacher looked up sharply, and Nellie

quickly pretended to be writing on her slate. After a moment she peeked sideways at Christy. Christy was staring at the hornet, her mouth open. The hornet shook out its wings and flew up to the top of Maud's head.

Christy's hand shot up in the air.

"What are you doing?" Nellie whispered, trying to pull it back down. She thought Christy was going to tell on her for whispering.

"Nellie, we must tell Teacher!" Christy whispered back.

"Girls, you know the rules about whispering," Teacher said, starting to walk toward them.

Just then Maud must have felt something on top of her head. She reached up to brush it away and let out a piercing shriek.

"Ow!" she screamed. "Ow! Ow!" She jumped up, shaking her hand.

"Maud!" Teacher said.

The girl next to Maud saw the hornet and screamed, too. She tried to climb over the girl next to her to get away. All the boys in the class jumped to their feet, trying to see what was happening.

Nellie laughed. She couldn't help it. Everyone looked so funny and alarmed with their eyes goggling out, when they had been so quiet and studious before. They were like a flock of startled geese.

"I got stung," Maud said, starting to cry.

"Nellie saw it," Christy said. "Nellie saw the hornet and didn't want me to tell. She wanted Maud to get stung."

"I did not!" said Nellie. This was mostly true. She had not cared whether Maud got stung or not. She had just wanted to see what would happen.

Teacher looked very stern.

"Nellie," she said, "it is wrong to laugh when other people get hurt."

"I wasn't laughing at *her*," Nellie tried to explain.

"Maud, come with me," said Teacher. "While I take care of Maud's hand, Nellie, I want you to go stand in the corner at the front of the room. Face the wall and think about how you would feel if you got stung and someone laughed at you. Stay there until I come back."

Nellie was so mad, she thought the top of her head might fly off. It wasn't fair! She hadn't done anything wrong!

But she didn't dare argue when Teacher looked so stern.

Nellie tossed her curls and lifted her chin. Her cheeks burned, but she would not show that she was embarrassed. She walked over to the corner with her head held high like a queen.

As Teacher left the room with Maud, Nellie could hear the other children start to whisper about her. She blinked as fast as she could, trying not to cry. It wasn't fair. It wasn't.

She stared hard at the line where the two walls met. Teacher would be sorry for punishing Nellie Oleson for no reason.

One way or another, Nellie was going to get even.

Making a Plan

All that day Nellie thought about how she would get her revenge on Teacher. After dinner, when Teacher called her and Christy up to read their letters, she put all her anger into her eyes. She stared and stared at Teacher as Christy stumbled over the words. She tried to look as mad and cold and righteous as possible. She thought of her father's face when Willie broke something in the store. She thought of her mother's face when one of them spilled milk on the rug. She tried to look that serious and angry.

She hoped Teacher could feel how much Nellie hated her. She hoped Teacher was starting to feel ashamed for punishing her.

Teacher did not look at her while Christy was reading. When Christy was finished, Teacher turned to Nellie and smiled. Nellie could not believe it. How dare she smile at Nellie! After what she'd done that morning!

Nellie did not smile back. She read her letters in an icy cold voice. When she was done, she shut her speller with a snap and glared at Teacher again.

"Very good, Nellie," Teacher said. "You may sit down."

Teacher acted as if she couldn't tell that Nellie was mad. It made Nellie want to scream and pull someone's hair. But she did not want to be punished again. She had to find a way to get revenge without getting caught.

At recess, Christy and Maud would not talk to Nellie. Maud had a bandage wrapped around her hand. The sting had swollen up so she could not hold a slate pencil. She would not be able to write for a few days.

Nellie didn't see what Maud was so mad about. Maud was lucky. She had not gotten in trouble for screaming during school. And now she had an excuse to skip her schoolwork until the swelling went down. Besides, it wasn't Nellie's fault. Maud was the one dumb enough to put her hand on a hornet.

And Christy was dumb, too, for thinking that Nellie didn't want her to tell about the hornet. Plus she was a tattletale. If anything, Nellie should be the one not speaking to *her*.

So instead of playing games with the other little girls, Nellie sat on the steps with the bigger girls, like Cassie Kennedy. Cassie's hair was not red like Christy's. It was black, like the hair on Nellie's china doll. She also had freckles, but not so many as Christy.

The big girls talked to one another. They did not have anything to say to Nellie. But Nellie listened and pretended they were talking to her, too. She felt quiet and ladylike sitting on the steps. It was shady and not as dusty here. Her mother would approve.

Nellie could hear the other girls shrieking as

they played on the side of the schoolhouse. None of them came to look for her, but she didn't care. She was the prettiest and the richest and the most popular girl in school. They would want to have her back soon.

In the meantime, she had revenge to plan.

Listening to the big girls gave her an idea.

"Did you hear about the Dawsons?" Emma asked Cassie. Emma was nearly ten. Her father was the town blacksmith. She had long brown hair that was so straight, it looked ironed. Nellie was glad Mrs. Oleson took the time to curl Nellie's hair. Emma's hair was very boring, in Nellie's opinion.

"The Dawsons?" Cassie said, shaking her head. "No, what happened? I saw that George wasn't in school."

"That's because they're gone," Emma said. "They moved back east."

Cassie looked surprised. "But they were here for only a year," she said.

"I know," Emma said. "I heard Ma and Pa talking. They said the Dawsons gave up. Their crops were bad and they had no money even for horseshoes. Prairie life was too hard for them. So they went home."

I wish we could go home, Nellie thought. *I wish I could go back east.* She didn't think prairie life was hard. She just thought it was boring and dirty.

"Who do you think will be next?" Cassie asked. She looked at the other students on the playground. "It seems like there's always someone new coming or going."

That gave Nellie her idea. Maybe she could make Teacher go back east, too. Maybe she could make the Beadles think life on the prairie was too hard. Maybe then they would give up and leave.

Then Nellie could get a new teacher—one who knew how special and pretty and important Nellie was.

Miss Beadle lived with her brother, Mr. Beadle. Neither of them were married. *I wouldn't want to marry them either*, Nellie thought. Mr. Beadle was already losing his hair. He was soft and pudgy around the middle, like a dumpling on legs. Even though he was a shopkeeper, which meant he was richer than a farmer, Nellie did not think he would find anyone to marry him, especially out here on the prairie.

The Beadles had arrived two years after the Olesons. Mr. Beadle had set up his shop and post office across the street from their store. Mr. Oleson grumbled about it a lot. He did not see the need for three stores in one town—his, Mr. Beadle's, and Mr. Fitch's. Neither did Nellie. Her father's store was the best, so why would anyone go anywhere else?

If Teacher and her brother left, that would be one less store in town. Nellie's father would surely be pleased by that.

But how could she scare them away? Nellie thought and thought. She thought of all the things she didn't like about the prairie. The dust. The constant wind. The wide-open sky with nothing to see. The insects everywhere.

Nellie narrowed her eyes. She was forming a plan. But she would need Willie's help.

After school, Teacher stood on the schoolhouse steps watching all the students leave. She smiled at each of them. She looked at Maud's hand and told her it would feel better soon.

Nellie did not look at Teacher. She turned up her nose and marched past her. But as she went down the path to town, she looked back. She saw Teacher closing the schoolhouse door securely behind her. There was no lock on the schoolhouse. Very few of the houses in town had locks on them, although of course the Olesons' store did.

Nellie smiled to herself.

Ahead of her she could see Christy and Maud walking together. Christy had her arm linked through Maud's, and their heads were leaning together. Christy's red hair and Maud's yellow hair looked like the red and yellow scrolls on the carpet in the Olesons' parlor. Nellie wondered if they were whispering about her.

I don't care, she told herself. *Maud is dull and mousy. Christy will be bored with her soon, and then she will want to be my friend again.*

Nellie flounced through the front door of the store, where both of her parents were working. Mr. and Mrs. Oleson were always too busy to talk to Nellie and Willie until supper. So Nellie and Willie were supposed to play by themselves.

After leaving his books at home, Willie usually ran outside to play with Sandy Kennedy and the other boys. But today Nellie followed him into the parlor and watched him drop his books on the floor in an untidy pile. Then she grabbed his arm before he could run off.

"Hey!" Willie yelled. "Let go!" He yanked on his arm, but Nellie had a fierce grip when she wanted something. "MA!" Willie hollered. "PA!"

"Stop yelling, you big baby," Nellie said. She wasn't worried about her parents coming in, because they were busy in the store. "Willie, I want you to do something."

Willie suddenly let himself go limp. He dropped his whole weight onto the carpeted floor of their parlor. But Nellie did not let go. She put both her hands around his wrist and stood over him. She made sure to stand away from his legs so he couldn't kick her. Willie was the kind of boy who *would* kick a girl.

"Let me go," he whined. "I want to go play."

"Willie," Nellie said, "do you want to do something wicked?"

Willie stopped whining. He sat up. His eyes were glinting with mischief. "What is it?" he asked. He squinted at her. "Is this a trick? Are you going to make me do something bad and then tell on me?"

Nellie shook her head. She let go of his arm. She knew she had his attention now.

"This is something bad we are going to do together," she said. "But if you tell on me, I will say it was your idea. You know everyone will believe me."

Willie knew that was true. He got in trouble all the time. But he liked making mischief. And he didn't mind getting dirty. Nellie was counting on that.

"Here's what I want you to do," Nellie said. She told Willie her plan. She thought it was a very good plan. Even Willie liked it. It was Willie's kind of trouble. But he wouldn't do it all by himself.

"You have to get me a jar," he said. "The glass kind with a lid that screws on."

Nellie knew where to find one of those. Her mother kept empty jars from the store in the lean-to off the parlor, where the iron cookstove and the pots and pans were. She used the jars when she made jam or preserved fruit.

Next to the stove there was a cabinet made of shiny brown wood. The two doors had tiny round button door knobs made of darker wood. The flat top of the cabinet was also a table for cutting and peeling and slicing food, so now it had knife marks flecking the surface like the scratches left in the dirt by prairie hens. But once, the wood had been smooth as water.

Nellie thought if she ever had something pretty like this cabinet, she wouldn't use it for messy things like cooking. She would keep pretty cups and saucers in it, and use the top as a table for serving tea and biscuits to her elegant high-society friends. All of them would wear long dresses and curl their hair, and none of them would be tattletales or cry over something silly like a hornet sting.

Nellie opened the cabinet and pulled out an empty jar. She was sure that her mother would never notice it was gone. Mr. and Mrs. Oleson kept track of every supply in the store, but once things were inside their own house, they didn't care so much about them. If they ever lost anything, they knew they could get another one from the store.

Nellie gave the jar to Willie.

"All right," Willie said with a grin. "Meet me by the lumber-yard in two hours."

Nellie grabbed his arm again. "Don't you tell anyone about this," she warned. "Not even Sandy. Or I will make you very sorry."

"Oh, shut up," Willie said. He shoved her away and ran back through the store to the street.

Nellie felt nervous. She could do nothing but wait. She went into the bedroom and tried to play with her doll, Laura, but she kept thinking about Teacher. She remembered standing in front of the room while everyone whispered about her. It wasn't fair, and she was going to get even.

She just hoped she didn't get caught.

The Empty Schoolhouse

It was nearly suppertime when Nellie and Willie met by the lumber-yard. She knew they would have to hurry to be back before their parents noticed they were gone. But it also meant that most people were inside at their own meals. No one would see them sneak off to the schoolhouse.

The schoolhouse was a little way outside of town, not on Main Street like their store. They stepped off the dusty street and onto the path that led to the schoolhouse. Tall prairie grass waved on either side of them. Nellie's heart was beating very fast. She looked behind her, but she saw no one.

"Come on, Willie, hurry up!" she said.

"I can't!" he said. "You don't want me to drop this, do you?"

Nellie looked at the jar he held between his hands. She shuddered to think of it breaking anywhere near her.

The sun was low in the sky. The prairie was so wide and flat that it wouldn't be fully dark until the sun was all the way down. The sky was streaked with dusky pink clouds, long and stretched out like taffy.

Nellie and Willie crept up to the school-house. It was deserted and shadowy. The closed door looked like the stern face of a reverend, all shut up tight and judging them. Nellie tossed back her curls. She would not be scared off by an empty schoolhouse. She marched up to the latch, lifted it, and pulled the door open.

"Quick, inside!" she whispered.

Willie grinned wickedly and stepped into the schoolhouse. Nellie followed him in and shut the door behind her. She didn't want anyone from the town spotting the open door and coming out to investigate.

The schoolhouse was spooky in the fading light. The two glass windows, normally open, were shut tight to keep out night animals. The room was quiet and still instead of being full of wind and light and buzzing noise the way it usually was. Nellie looked up at the ceiling, where orange light from the setting sun ran crookedly across the undersides of the shingles.

"All right," she said. "Go ahead and do it."

Willie looked at her like she'd just set her own head on fire. "I did my part," he said. "*You* do it."

"I can't!" Nellie said. "You have to. Hurry up."

Willie set the jar on the nearest bench and crossed his arms. He made a stubborn face. "This was your plan. *You* have to do it."

"Willie!" Nellie cried. "I can't touch those horrid things. I don't want to be anywhere near them."

"Maybe I should just break the jar right here, then," Willie said. He picked up the jar and held it in the air like he was going to drop it.

"Oh, don't!" Nellie squealed, jumping back. "I'll do it, I will—just don't break it."

Willie lowered the jar with a smug smile. He held it out to her.

Nellie shivered. But she was determined to do this. Teacher deserved it.

She took the jar from Willie, holding it as far away from her as she could. She walked to the front of the room, to the platform where Teacher sat during the day. Her footsteps in her shoes sounded very loud in the stillness. *Clop, clop, clop.*

Teacher kept her books and slate and ruler inside her desk. The top of the desk lifted up on hinges that had come from Mr. Beadle's store. Nellie had seen Mr. Beadle smoothing the wood to make the desk. He had given the school many things from his store for free because his sister was the teacher. Nellie thought that was not fair. If Mr. Beadle had not given the schoolhouse chalk and slates and boughten hinges, the school board would have had to buy them. And maybe they would have bought them from her father's store.

Nellie set the jar down very slowly on Teacher's chair.

"Willie," she whispered. "Will you at least come hold the desk open for me?"

Willie came up to the platform, his hands jammed into his pockets. He jumped up on one of the front benches and walked along it.

"This is fun," he said. "I should sneak into the schoolhouse again. I like it when there's no one to yell at me for standing on the benches." He jumped down and skipped over to the blackboard.

"Stop it, Willie," Nellie said. "I want to do this quick and go home."

Willie ignored her. He picked up a piece of chalk and wrote: TEECHER IS A COW in big scraggly letters. Then he dusted off his hands and walked up to Teacher's desk.

"Hold the desk open while I unscrew the jar," Nellie said.

Willie lifted the top of the desk. Inside, Teacher's things were lined up neatly. There were two stacks of books. Her ruler was at the edge nearest her hands, so she could reach it quickly when she needed to rap for order or slap someone's knuckles as a punishment. Her slate and slate pencil were on top of one of the piles of books. All the edges were lined up perfectly.

Seeing everything so neat made Nellie mad all over again. Teacher was so proper and so calm about everything. She never yelled. She just made you feel awful and small with one look. Nellie wanted to see Teacher upset. She wanted to break the porcelain smoothness of Teacher's expression. She wanted to see Teacher be as angry as Nellie was.

Quickly, Nellie moved everything around in the desk. She mixed up the piles of books and left them in untidy heaps. She dropped the slate pencil on the floor and stamped on it so it broke in half. Then she hid both halves along with the ruler at the back of the desk.

Next she lifted the jar off the chair. She carefully unscrewed the lid and held the jar out as far as she could. She pulled off the top and turned the jar upside down.

All the bugs and other disgusting things Willie had been able to find poured out into

Teacher's desk. There were water bugs and grasshoppers, flies and crickets. There were long-legged stick insects and shiny green beetles. There were tiny brown spiders and furry caterpillars. Nellie had to shake loose two earthworms and a snail that were stuck to the bottom. Her skin crawled as she thought of any of these creatures touching her.

She jumped back and Willie slammed the top of the desk down, trapping the insects inside. The last thing Nellie saw was a bunch of squirming, wriggling legs scattering over the piles of books.

"Teacher will be sorry now," Nellie said.

She felt proud of herself. She had come up with a clever plan. Teacher would be terribly frightened, and the whole school day would be disrupted. Nellie and Willie would never get caught. And she had been brave enough to open the jar herself. She was braver than she thought.

Nellie fastened the door securely behind them as they left. She hid the jar in her apron to carry it home. Then she hid it behind the log pile. She could get the jar and wash it later, but if she tried to bring it in now, her mother might notice.

Willie stopped her before they went into the store.

"We should make a pact," he said.

"What kind of pact?" asked Nellie.

"If one of us gets caught, we don't tell on the other," Willie said. "That means if you get caught, don't squeal on me."

"Same to you!" Nellie said. "You better not tell on me if you get in trouble."

"Deal," Willie said. He spat on his hand and held it out to her.

"That's vile, Willie," Nellie said.

Willie sighed and wiped off his hand on his shirt. "Girls," he muttered. Then he held his hand out again and she shook it, dropping it quickly.

"Deal," Nellie said. She marched inside to wash her hands. She was pleased. No one would ever think that pretty, perfect Nellie Oleson would do something wicked and horrid involving insects. If anyone did get in trouble, it would be Willie.

She used the china pitcher in the bedroom to pour water into the china bowl. Then she scrubbed and scrubbed her hands with soap from the little china dish. She had not touched any insects herself, but she felt like her skin was still crawling with them.

She could smell salt pork frying in the kitchen lean-to. She had seen her mother mashing potatoes as she went through the parlor. She knew they would have meat and buttery potatoes tonight. Thank goodness her father was a storekeeper. She wondered what Teacher was eating. Surely Mr. Beadle wasn't as rich as the Olesons.

Nellie wiped her hands dry on a blue-and-white checkered cloth. She smiled at herself in the big looking-glass and tossed her curls. She couldn't wait for school tomorrow. She couldn't wait to see Teacher scream when she opened her desk. It was going to be a wonderful revenge.

Beetles for Miss Beadle

Nellie hurried through getting dressed and eating breakfast so she could get to school early. Even Willie did not dawdle around the store eating candy. They both went quickly up the street and through the long grass to the schoolhouse. It was not a sunny day like the one before. Gray clouds were piling up in the sky. The breeze carried a hint of cold and rain in it.

Teacher was standing outside on the steps. She gave Nellie and Willie a curious look, as if she was surprised to see them so early. But she did not look mad. She must not have opened her desk yet.

Nellie could barely sit still as all the other students came in. It seemed to take forever for them to take their places. Christy and Maud sat next to each other and did not look at her, but Nellie did not care.

She pretended to be studying her reader as Teacher went past her to the front of the room. She heard Teacher's shoes tapping on the wooden floor.

Teacher reached her desk and turned around. "Good morning, class," she said.

"Good morning, Teacher," the children chorused.

"I think we shall begin today with a spelling test," Teacher said. Nellie held her breath. This was the moment! Teacher walked around her desk and opened the top to get out her speller. She stopped. She gazed into her desk for a moment and then quickly shut it again.

But she did not scream. She did not even look shocked. She only looked thoughtful.

Nellie was tremendously disappointed. This

was not the terrified reaction she had been hoping for.

"Or perhaps," Teacher said, "we will begin with a science project." She put both of her hands on top of her desk. "It seems that a number of insects have gotten into my desk during the night. I want each of you to come up and catch one insect from inside here. Then you will tell me what kind of insect it is, and you will go release it outside. Understand?"

Nellie was horrified. Surely Teacher didn't mean that they had to *touch* the insects . . . with their *hands*?

"Hopefully we will all learn a little about the creatures we share the earth with. Who would like to go first?" Teacher asked.

Sandy Kennedy's hand shot up in the air.

"All right, Sandy, come up here."

Sandy bounded out of his chair and up to the platform at the front of the room. Teacher said, "Ready?" and he nodded. She lifted the lid of her desk and he looked inside. His eyes goggled. He looked flabbergasted. That was more like the reaction Nellie had wanted from Teacher.

"Quickly, Sandy," Teacher said. Sandy reached into the desk and cupped his hands around something. He lifted it out, keeping his hands close together so it couldn't escape. Teacher shut the desk again.

"Now, Sandy, what do you have in your hands?" Teacher asked.

"This is a cricket," Sandy said.

"That's right," said Teacher. "Did you know that crickets are sometimes kept as pets in China?"

"Really?" said Sandy in an amazed voice.

"Yes," said Teacher. "The Chinese consider them to be good luck."

"Wow!" Sandy said.

"All right, you may take the cricket outside and release it gently," said Teacher. "Then come right back in."

Sandy went down the aisle to the door, holding the cricket carefully between his hands. One of the bigger boys at the back jumped up to open the door for him.

"Who's next?" Teacher asked.

"Me!" Willie yelled, raising his hand.

"Shhh," Teacher said. "Quietly, Willie, come forward."

Willie ran to Teacher's desk. Nellie was disgusted with him. He didn't seem to remember the revenge plan at all. He didn't care that Teacher wasn't upset about the bugs. He just couldn't wait to grab one for himself.

Before Teacher could lift the lid, Willie shouted, "I want the earthworm!"

She paused and looked at him. "What makes you think there's an earthworm in here?" she asked.

Willie was so dumb! Nellie shook her head. Of course he would give away that he knew about the bugs. She only hoped that he would remember the pact and not give her away, too.

"I just . . ." Willie stammered. "Well, isn't there?"

"Let's find out," Teacher said. She lifted the lid, and Willie stuck his head inside. He reached into the desk and triumphantly held up a long, squirmy, pinkish-gray earthworm.

Teacher closed the desk again.

"This is an earthworm!" Willie announced.

Nellie felt ill. She couldn't do this. She couldn't go up there and hold something like that in her hands. She'd never seen anything so disgusting.

"Earthworms are very good for the garden," Teacher said. "They keep the soil fertile so plants can grow. Now take it outside, Willie."

Willie paraded to the door. As he passed Nellie, he waggled the earthworm at her. She shrieked and scrambled to the far end of the bench.

After that, everyone was eager to volunteer. Christy went up next and rescued a shiny green beetle. Maud got one of the hairy caterpillars. She squealed and giggled about how it was tickling her, but she managed to get it safely outside.

Nellie hoped and hoped that the desk would run out of bugs before they got to her. She sat on her hands and waited as one by one the students volunteered. She watched them go by with insects cupped between their hands.

But she soon ran out of luck. Teacher looked straight at her and said, "Nellie, everyone has gone but you. It is your turn."

"I can't!" Nellie said.

"Yes, you can," Teacher said. "And you have to. This is your assignment."

Nellie dragged herself to her feet. She walked as slowly as possible up to the front of the room. She stood an arm's length away from Teacher's desk.

"Get ready," said Teacher, and she lifted the top of the desk.

It was not as messy inside as Nellie remembered. Most of the insects were gone now. She could see something moving behind one pile of books. She also saw that one of the earthworms had gotten squashed at the bottom of the desk. She shuddered. She would *never* pick up a dead earthworm.

"Go ahead, Nellie," Teacher said.

Nellie reached slowly into the desk and pulled back the pile of books. A large green grasshopper sat at the back of the desk. It stared at her with enormous, bulging eyes. And then, all at once, it leaped into her hands.

Nellie was too astonished to scream. She hadn't expected the creature to come to her so easily. She quickly put one hand over the other so the grasshopper was trapped in between. She could feel its hairy, long legs brushing against her palms. It made her want to shake herself all over to get the feeling of prickles out from under her skin.

"And what is that, Nellie?" Teacher asked.

"It's a grasshopper," Nellie said. "Please can I let go of it?"

"Outside," Teacher said, pointing. "Don't let it go in here."

Nellie ran as fast as she could. She ran down the aisle to the door, which the boy held open again. She ran out onto the schoolhouse steps and threw her hands open, flinging the grasshopper free.

The grasshopper flew through the air and landed on the dirt in front of the schoolhouse. It sat for a minute as if it was stunned. Then it jumped forward, and forward again, and disappeared into the long grass.

Nellie rubbed and rubbed her hands together to get the feeling of the prickly insect legs off them. It had not been as awful as she'd expected, but it had not been nice, either. This was not how she had wanted the morning to go. Teacher was too clever.

She went back inside and sat down.

"Well done, everyone," said Teacher. She beckoned to the two biggest boys. "Donald and James, please carry my desk outside and make sure there are no more insects left in it. In the meanwhile, the rest of us shall go ahead with the spelling test. Everyone get your slates and slate pencils ready."

Nellie sighed. It was back to class as normal. Teacher hadn't punished anyone, not even Willie, who had known there was an earthworm in her desk. She didn't seem to care that her desk was full of bugs. Nellie's plan had not worked at all.

GRASSHOPPER WEATHER

Nellie wrote her name at the top of the slate in wobbly, curvy letters, as Teacher told them to. She wrote down each word as Teacher said it. It was a funny test. Most of the words were creatures: CRICKET, SPIDER, WORM. Some of the words were normal: SLATE, DESK, TEACHER. Nellie tried to write neatly. She was usually good at spelling.

Then Teacher collected their slates and told them all to open their readers and work quietly for a few moments while she sat down to review the tests. Nellie sneaked a glance at Willie, who was kicking the back of the bench in front of him. He was not studying in his reader.

Finally, Teacher set the slates aside. She stood up with a serious look on her face.

"Willie Oleson," she said. "Please come with me. The rest of you stay seated until I return."

She walked out of the schoolhouse. Willie looked frightened. Nellie shook her head at him and mouthed the words, "The pact!" If he was going to get in trouble, Nellie wanted to make sure he didn't squeal on her.

Willie scrambled after Teacher. They were gone for a long time. Everyone was very still. They could tell Willie was probably in trouble, although they did not know why. Nobody else wanted to get in trouble.

Finally Teacher came back without Willie. She did not say where he was or why she had taken him away. She gave all their slates back and called up the oldest students for math review.

Nellie did not find out what had happened until she went home at midday for dinner. She found Willie dusting in the store. Mr. Oleson was watching him with an angry expression.

"Teacher brought me home," Willie said. "She told Pa that I snuck into the school."

"How did she know?" Nellie asked. "Because of what you said about the earthworm?"

"And my spelling," Willie said. "I guess I don't know how to spell 'Teacher.'" Suddenly Nellie remembered what Willie had written on the board. They had forgotten to erase it before leaving. Teacher must have found it and erased it when she went into the schoolhouse in the morning. That was why she had used it in the spelling test. She was looking for the person who spelled it "Teecher." That was how she had caught Willie.

"Have you been expelled?" Nellie asked.

"No," Willie said grumpily. "I just have to stay home today and do all these chores. And Father said he'll be keeping an eye on me in the afternoons from now on. He also offered to give her a lock from the store for free."

"Oooh," Nellie said. "I bet he didn't like that."

Willie shook his head. "This isn't fair," he whispered. "They should be mad at *you*."

Nellie smiled sweetly. "But you promised, Willie," she said. "We made a pact."

"I know," Willie said. "But it's still not fair."

"Nellie," Mr. Oleson called, "leave Willie to do his work and go eat your dinner."

"Yes, Father," she said, tossing her curls. She danced back to the parlor, feeling pleased with herself. Now everyone would blame Willie. Her plan hadn't worked out perfectly . . . but at least she hadn't been caught.

Christy and Maud forgot about being mad at Nellie after a few days. Maud's hand healed, and they all went back to playing games together in the school yard.

Willie sulked for a week and was horrible to Nellie the whole time. He ripped three of her paper dolls and pulled all the stitching out of her needlepoint sampler. But he did not tell on her. He had a strange sense of honor when it came to making trouble.

But still, Nellie was not happy. She did not feel triumphant about the trick she had played on Teacher. And she was afraid that Teacher knew she had planned it. Sometimes Nellie would look up and find Teacher watching her with a disappointed expression. Teacher did not smile at her the way she used to. She did not say that Nellie was doing a good job.

Nellie tried to tell herself that she did not care. She didn't want to be Teacher's friend, anyway. But part of her began to wish she had not tried to get revenge on Teacher.

A couple of months later, school closed for the winter, although the weather stayed warm and dry all the way to November. There was no frost and no snow and no rain. Just clear, sun-filled days and chilly nights.

The colder it got, the more men came into the store to gather around the stove and talk. They smoked their pipes and exchanged news. This was how information traveled. Nellie would almost always find at least three men talking with her father about crops and politics and trains and the new buildings that were going up in town. Nellie did not care about any of those things. She thought their conversations were more boring than anything she could imagine. She avoided the groups of men as much as possible, and so did Mrs. Oleson.

One day the stranger from before came into the store again—the man named Charles Ingalls. This time he brought his wife and a small girl in pink calico and a pink sunbonnet, with long golden curls like Nellie's. Mr. Ingalls introduced them as Caroline Ingalls and his daughter Carrie. Mrs. Oleson politely shook their hands and admired Mrs. Ingalls' nice dress. She did not *sniff-sniff* the way she did at most people in town. Later she said that Caroline Ingalls seemed more cultured and well-bred than the other women in Walnut Grove.

Nellie stayed in the back while they were in the store. She did not want to meet any new people. She also did not like seeing another little girl as pretty as she was, even if the other girl was so much younger than Nellie.

Mr. Ingalls bought many supplies from their store. He saw the men standing around the stove and joined their talk.

"Funny weather we're having, isn't it?" one of them said.

"Sure beats the early frost we had last year,"

said another. "I wouldn't mind if it stayed like this for the whole winter."

"I heard the old-timers call it 'grasshopper weather,'" said Mr. Ingalls. "Any idea why?"

The men shook their heads. "I've heard that, too," said Mr. Oleson. "But it doesn't mean anything to me."

"Charles, we should take something back for Laura and Mary," Mrs. Ingalls said.

"Of course," he agreed. "Which candy would you recommend, Oleson?"

Nellie's father showed Mr. Ingalls the various kinds of candy he had. He pointed out the horehound candy sticks that Nellie loved. "My little girl is particularly fond of those," he said.

"Then I'm sure our daughters will like them," Mr. Ingalls said. "We'll take three sticks."

Nellie peeked out from behind the shelves. She wondered how old Laura and Mary were. She hoped they weren't her age. She didn't like it when new children came to the school. But perhaps it was too far for them to come, anyway. Perhaps they would stay out in the country, where they belonged.

THE NUTCRACKER

Nellie knew that girls like Christy Kennedy got excited about Thanksgiving and Christmas. For them a holiday was not like any other day. On Thanksgiving they ate roast goose or turkey. On Christmas they got special presents. If they were lucky, they got candy, which Mr. Kennedy came to buy at the Olesons' store.

Nellie saw Mr. Kennedy buying candy this year, a week before Christmas. There were five children in his family: Christy, who was Nellie's age; Sandy, who was Willie's age; two older girls, Nettie and Cassie, and another older boy, Donald. That was a lot of people to buy presents for. Nellie saw Mr. Kennedy take a small pile of candy and divide it into five smaller piles. Then Nellie's father took one small pile and put it in the center of a square of brown paper. He folded the paper up and, with a quick twist of his hands, he made a tiny package of candy. He did this with each pile until Mr. Kennedy had five paper packages.

They looked very small to Nellie. She ate that much candy every day, whenever she wanted to. She could not imagine eating a tiny package of candy only once a year. She would hate to be poor.

She was glad she didn't have a huge pile of brothers and sisters. She wouldn't want to share her candy with anybody else.

Nellie did not think that Christmas was as thrilling as everyone made it out to be. She could have anything she wanted any day of the year. And her family ate beef or turkey or goose whenever they felt like it. So what was so special about this one day?

As far as Nellie could tell, all it meant was that her parents would close the shop and sit in the parlor all day, like they did on Sundays. Mr. Oleson would smoke his pipe and rock back and forth in his rocking chair. He didn't like closing the store, not even for Christmas, but Mrs. Oleson said he had to. She said it wouldn't be proper if he didn't. So he sat and rocked, and her mother sat and sewed or read magazines like *Godey's Lady's Book* or *Peterson's Magazine*.

Nellie did like the presents part of Christmas. She liked opening the mysterious packages and finding exciting new toys inside. She liked the surprise when it was something she hadn't seen in the store.

But after the presents Willie and Nellie would have to be quiet all the rest of the day. Willie always forgot by afternoon and got into mischief, and then her father would yell and her mother would be angry and they'd be sent to the bedroom until suppertime.

Christmas was not very much fun in the Oleson house.

Christy Kennedy came into the store with

her mother two days before Christmas. Nellie had been dusting the shelves, but when she heard the front door swing open and felt the cold air fly in, she hid her rag inside a dinner pail. She tried to act as if she had just come in from the back herself.

Christy was bundled up in a green coat with gold-colored buttons that looked like tiny engraved shields. The dark-green wool made her hair look even brighter, like fire in a pine forest. Sparkling white dots of snow freckled her hair, and as she stood in the doorway, Nellie could see them melting into dark wet spots.

"Hi, Nellie," Christy said breathlessly, unwinding her pale-green woolen scarf. "Oooh, it's cold outside." She stamped her feet on the mat by the door. Nellie saw flecks of snow and dirt fly off and land on the floor. She scowled. She knew her father would make her mop the floor later.

"Hello, Nellie," Mrs. Kennedy said, patting Nellie's head. "My, your hair is shiny. How does your mother keep it so clean?" Nellie liked being admired, but she didn't like having her head patted. She tossed her curls and stepped back out of reach.

"We are very clean in *our* household," she said primly.

Mrs. Kennedy did not seem to notice that she'd been insulted. She stepped past Nellie to the counter and asked Mr. Oleson if she could see a selection of ribbons. Nellie guessed she was putting the finishing touches on a present for one of the girls.

Christy shook her head, her red braids flying and scattering drops of melting snow. Her cheeks were pink with cold, so all her freckles stood out. She went over to the stove in the middle of the store and stood warming her hands.

"Aren't you ever so excited about Christmas, Nellie?" Christy asked in her chattering way. "I've been counting down the days. Ma helped me make a new bonnet for Cassie. I can't wait until she sees it. It's red, so it will be pretty with her black hair. And for Sandy, Nettie and I knitted him new mittens. I did part of the hands, and she did the hard part around the thumbs. I can't wait to give them to him! What are you giving Willie?"

Nellie had not thought of giving Willie a present. He would get plenty of presents from Mother and Father. And he certainly would not be giving Nellie a present. But Christy was looking at her with her large, dark-blue eyes. Nellie knew Christy would not understand if Nellie said she was not giving Willie anything.

"Oh," Nellie said, "I'll just give him any old thing from in here. My father won't mind. We can take what we like. Maybe this." She picked up a nutcracker from a nearby shelf. It was made of wood and carved to look like a soldier in a bright-red coat, white trousers, and tall black boots. Tufts of white hair stuck out from under his cap, and more hair was fixed to his chin to make a beard. The white hair did not match his black eyebrows and mustache, but it was very soft, like a fur muff. A lever on his back made the little man's mouth open and close very wide. If you put a nut in his mouth and pushed the lever down, it would crack the nutshell.

The nutcracker was in a section of Christmas items that had come in on the train from

back east a month ago. Nellie had been looking at it ever since, but she knew it wasn't ladylike to want to play with a soldier doll. Still,
she liked to pick it up and lift the lever up and
down. The nutcracker's face looked very
solemn and fierce, but opening its mouth so
wide made it look silly. She liked watching the
change—solemn, silly, solemn, silly. Perhaps if
she gave it to Willie, she would be able to play
with it sometimes, too.

"That's very nice," Christy said politely.
"I'm sure he will like it."

"I wonder what *I* will get," Nellie said. She
set the nutcracker back on the shelf.

"I wonder, too," Christy said. "I have no
idea what my presents will be."

Nellie knew what she wanted. She wanted a
horse of her own. She wanted a shiny brown
horse with a long dark mane and slender legs.
She wanted a neat little sleigh for it to pull her
around in. But there was nowhere for them to
keep a horse. Her parents did not need a horse,
because they were prosperous storekeepers, not
farmers who needed horses for farmwork. And

she was too young to have a horse of her own. So she had to pretend that she did not want one.

"I expect I shall get another doll," Nellie said. "I am sure it will be the prettiest doll anyone in this town has ever seen. My aunt Laura always sends me elegant presents from back east." Impulsively, she added, "One day we'll go back there. We're not going to stay here forever."

"Go back?" Christy said. "Why would you want to? All the new excitement is out west. I want to keep going, all the way to the other side of the country."

"Not me," Nellie said with a shudder. "The best people are all in New York. The most fashionable clothes and the most beautiful parks and the most wonderful tall buildings. That is where I should live, where it isn't so horrid and dusty."

"It's not dusty here right now," Christy said cheerfully. "All the dust is buried under the snow."

Nellie rolled her eyes. She looked over at Mrs. Kennedy and her father. Mr. Oleson had his for-customers-only smile on his face. He was laying out strand after strand of ribbon—thin pink silk ribbon, wide blue-and-yellow flannel ribbon, red ribbon trimmed with lace, pale lavender ribbon printed with dark purple flowers.

"I hunted through our house," Nellie whispered to Christy, "but I couldn't find where Mother hid our presents this year."

Christy looked shocked. "Nellie Oleson!" she exclaimed. "Why would you do such a thing? Goodness, you'll ruin Christmas for yourself that way."

"No, I won't," Nellie said. She felt herself starting to get mad. She'd told Christy a secret, and now Christy was acting like a bossy grown-up about it. "It's just the same to find out now or two days from now. The presents will still be mine. My parents don't care."

"They must care a little if they've hidden them so well," Christy pointed out. "I wouldn't want to know what *I* was getting."

"You're getting candy," Nellie said spitefully. "The wavy ribbon kind. I saw your father buying it a few days ago."

Christy's mouth dropped open. Nellie thought that she looked a bit like the nutcracker at his silliest. She wanted to pop a nut into her mouth and see if Christy could crack it like the nutcracker did.

"Nellie Oleson, that is just mean!" Christy said. "I told you I didn't want to know, and you told me anyway!"

"Oh, you must have known you'd get candy in your stocking," Nellie said.

"I did not know, and I didn't want to know," Christy said stoutly. Nellie could tell that Christy was secretly excited about the candy, but she was trying not to show it. It seemed pointless to Nellie. Now Christy could be excited about candy for two whole days. And anyway, it came from Nellie's father's store. She should be allowed to talk about it if she wanted.

"Well, surely that won't be your *only* present," Nellie said. "Your family isn't *that* poor."

Christy's cheeks were as bright pink as they had been when she walked in from the cold. She bit her lip and looked as if she wanted to say something else.

"All right, Christy, let's go," Mrs. Kennedy said from the door. Christy hurried over to her mother, winding her scarf back around her head. "Say Merry Christmas to Nellie, dear," Mrs. Kennedy said.

"Merry Christmas, Nellie," Christy mumbled.

"Merry Christmas, Christy," Nellie said with a fake smile. "I hope it's a very *sweet* one."

Christy blinked and followed her mother quickly out the door.

Nellie snatched the nutcracker up and stomped back through the store into their parlor. Her mother was at the table doing accounts.

"I want this," Nellie said, banging the nutcracker down on the table.

Her mother looked over her spectacles at the nutcracker. "Hmm," she said. She pulled one of her ledgers toward her and began to flip through it. Nellie knew that she was checking on the price they had paid for the nutcracker.

"To give to Willie," Nellie added quickly. "For Christmas."

Her mother looked astonished. "You want to give Willie a Christmas present?" Mrs. Oleson asked.

Nellie widened her eyes. "Don't you think I

should, Ma?" she said in her sweetest voice. "It seems like a good, charitable thing to do."

"Why, yes it is, dear," Mrs. Oleson said. She patted Nellie's hand, but her eyes were already moving back to the pages in front of her.

"Then you must wrap it for me," Nellie said. She shoved the nutcracker in front of her mother and flounced back to the bedroom.

She wondered what Willie would think of the nutcracker. She wondered how long it would take until he got bored with it and she could sneak it away from him. The nutcracker was smaller than her doll, Laura, but they would look very fine next to each other. The nutcracker could be Laura's dashing escort to fancy balls and high-society parties.

She got Laura out from her drawer and began to tell her stories about her fabulous future life as Mrs. Nutcracker.

She forgot all about the dusting, and about the rag she had hidden in the dinner pail, until two weeks later, when Mr. Oleson found it as he was selling the pail to a customer. He scolded Nellie, but as usual, she did not listen.

AN ORDINARY CHRISTMAS

On Christmas morning Nellie was awakened early by the sounds of Willie banging through the house.

"It's Christmas, it's Christmas!" he sang out from the parlor.

"Willie, be quiet and go back to sleep!" Mr. Oleson yelled from his bed.

Willie ignored him. "Presents, presents!" he shouted. "I see lumps in my stocking!"

"It'll be lumps of coal if you don't leave us in peace for another hour!" Mr. Oleson threatened.

There was silence for a few minutes. Nellie

knew that Willie had not gone back to bed. He was quietly digging through his stocking and shaking his Christmas boxes. If she did not get out there quickly, he would move on to her stocking next.

She stuck one foot out of the bed. Brrr! Her toes felt frozen. They would have to stay that way until her parents woke up. Neither she nor Willie was allowed to start the fire in the stove.

Nellie swung her legs over the edge of the bed and yawned. She wrapped her blue flowered quilt around herself as tight as she could and went into the parlor, the edge of the quilt dragging on the floor behind her like a queen's robe.

Willie had his grubby fingers all over her stocking, poking the lumps as he tried to figure out what they were.

"Willie!" she yelled. "That's MINE!"

He jumped a foot.

"I wasn't doing anything!" he protested.

"You were going to steal my candy!" she said.

"No, I wasn't!"

"BE QUIET!" Mr. Oleson roared.

Willie covered his mouth with both hands.

Nellie made a horrible face at him. She dragged the quilt over and pushed aside the lacy white curtain to look out the window. The sun was about to rise. The wooden buildings and the snow-covered street outside were still all the same colorless gray of the time right before dawn, but golden edges of light were starting to appear along the rooftops. Nellie could not see anyone awake yet.

"Willie," she whispered in disgust, "it's too early to be awake."

"I want my presents now," Willie said stubbornly.

"We're not going to get anything if you don't stop being such a monster," Nellie hissed. She sat down on the carpet and leaned against one of the round table legs. She didn't dare go back to bed and leave Willie alone with her candy. So she just had to wait until her parents woke up, too.

She stared up at the paintings on the wall. Her favorite was a painting of the Hudson River, which ran through New York State and alongside the island of Manhattan. Although you could not see the city in the painting, she knew it was just beyond the craggy cliffs and white birch trees. Tall ships were sailing along the river. Nellie imagined that they were carrying barrels and crates overflowing with strange fruit, toys from faraway lands, and exotic animals like monkeys and toucans, which she had seen pictures of in a book.

Nellie loved boxes, especially mysterious ones that were packed with new things. Every time her father got supplies on the train from back east, she watched him open the crates and unpack everything into the store. It was the only chore she did not mind helping with.

She liked to see what was new back in New York. She liked to be the first one to open the magazines and see the new dress styles. She liked to be the first one to touch the new bolts of cloth and smooth wooden jewelry boxes.

Nellie must have dozed off, because when she woke up again, she was curled on her side with her face pressed into the thick, rough carpet. She pushed herself up quickly and rubbed her face, knowing she must have a prickly pink imprint on her cheek. Willie was asleep again, too, curled awkwardly in their mother's armchair with one arm hanging off the side and his blond hair sticking up in spikes.

The sun was finally coming in through the window, dappling the floor in sunny patches through the lace of the curtain.

Nellie rubbed her hands together. She could see the faint wisp of her own breath in the air. She was starting to feel hungry. She wondered if her parents would notice if she took some of the candy out of her stocking and ate it. Or perhaps she should go into the store and get some from one of the barrels in there.

Just then she heard movement from the bedroom. Nellie scrambled to her feet and patted the curl-papers on her head to make sure she hadn't squashed them.

Mrs. Oleson came out of the bedroom dressed in her dark-gray wool dress. Silver buttons ran down the front, and in the back the dress was tucked and lifted into elegant drapes and puffs. Nellie couldn't wait until she could wear dresses that beautiful. Her mother also wore a soft white crocheted shawl over her shoulders, keeping her warm. Nellie watched as she hurried over to the stove and lit it.

"Oh, Nellie," her mother said, noticing her. "Bring me some water to boil for tea."

"Why can't Willie do it?" Nellie complained. "It's cold outside."

"Wear your gloves," her mother said. "Hurry now—your father is waiting."

Nellie shoved her feet into her boots, pulled on her coat, and stomped out the back to the pump. Her ears instantly felt cold as ice, like they were thin as bone china and about to snap off in the freezing air.

The pump was frozen solid, and Nellie had to kick it several times before it would move enough for her to get water out. She carried the full kettle back inside. Although she tried not to spill, some water dripped on the wooden floor of the lean-to.

"Here, mop that up," Mrs. Oleson said, taking the kettle and handing Nellie a rag.

Grouchily, Nellie wiped the rag over the floor. Then, before her mother could give her anything else to do, she stamped over and pinched Willie's arm to wake him up.

"OW!" Willie yelped, sitting up quickly.

"Stop yelling," Mr. Oleson said, coming into the room. "And for goodness' sake, go get dressed. Is this a household of heathens?"

"Merry Christmas!" Willie sang out. "Merry Christmas! Time for presents!"

"Not until you're both dressed," their father said firmly.

Nellie and Willie rushed into the bedroom and changed quickly into regular clothes. They wanted to get back out to the parlor for presents, but they also hurried because it was so cold.

Nellie was finished first, and she ran triumphantly into the parlor. "I'm ready!" she cried. "I'm ready first!"

"Nellie, come here," her mother said. She unwound Nellie's curl-papers and brushed Nellie's hair into shining ringlets. Then she tied an apron over Nellie's pretty red wool dress.

"You can help me with the pancakes," she said.

"Presents first!" Willie demanded.

"You may have your stockings," Mr. Oleson said, "but no presents until after breakfast."

As Nellie had expected, her stocking was full of candy. At the bottom was a round red apple. There was also a pair of tiny carved wooden dolls, a boy and a girl, with matching round red circles on their cheeks and tiny fingernails delicately carved on their hands.

Willie got a new whistle in his stocking, which Nellie knew right away was a bad idea. Sure enough, he started blowing on it and kept up an ear-piercing racket the entire time Nellie and her mother were making the pancakes, even though their father told him to stop several times.

Most of the time Nellie hated helping in the kitchen. It was nice and warm right by the stove, but usually it was too hot on one side of her and too cold on the other. She always spilled something on her apron and her hands and the floor and the counter, and then she had to clean it up. Her mother was very strict about exact measurements, so Nellie was often scolded for mistakes like heaping the cup of flour too high.

But sometimes she liked it. When her mother was feeling calm and unhurried, it could be peaceful in the kitchen. If Nellie did things right, sometimes her mother would tell her she'd done well. And the smell of baking usually made Nellie feel less mad.

Of course, today the screeching of Willie's whistle didn't help her mother feel calm, and it didn't let Nellie feel peaceful, either. It just made her grumpy, which made her think about how much work everything was out here on the prairie. In New York surely everything would be easier.

Nellie brought her mother the ingredients as Mrs. Oleson asked for them. From the sacks of flour, Mrs. Oleson carefully measured out exactly one cup of white flour and one cup of whole wheat flour. Then she sent Nellie to the pantry to get buttermilk, salt, and an egg.

The pantry was a separate room Mr. Oleson had built right outside the back door. It wasn't really big enough to be called a room. It was just a set of shelves with a door, but at night Mr. Oleson locked it up so no one could get in to steal their food. This was where the Olesons kept their milk and things like tea and salt. It was cooler out there, farther away from the stove, so everything would last longer.

Nellie used a dipper to measure out two cups of buttermilk into a pitcher. She carried it carefully back into the house, and this time she did not spill any. Her mother added the buttermilk, salt, an egg, and saleratus to the flour mixture. She gave Nellie a wooden spoon.

"Stir it all together," Mrs. Oleson said. "Make sure there aren't any lumps of flour left. Willie! Would you please keep quiet!"

Tweeeeeeeeeeeet! went Willie's whistle.

Nellie stirred and stirred until her arm hurt. She wished Willie had to do something useful, instead of sitting there blowing his horrid whistle.

Mrs. Oleson set the flat iron griddle on top of the cookstove. As it heated, she sprinkled water on the griddle until the droplets jumped and sizzled. That meant the griddle was hot enough. Then she used salt pork fat to grease it.

"All right," she said, taking the bowl away

from Nellie. "Go get me the butter from the pantry, and then you and your brother can set the table."

Nellie and her mother had churned the butter the day before, Thursday, so there was fresh yellow butter pressed into the wooden butter molds in the pantry. Nellie hated churning, but she liked the way the butter looked when they were done. She chose a butter mold that was round with a sunflower shape carved on it. Carefully she pressed the pat of butter out of the mold and onto a small china dish. Now it looked like a round gold coin with a sunflower stamped in the middle. And it was only a little dented around the edges. Nellie tried to poke them back into a smooth round shape, but she just made them messier and left fingerprints in the butter, so she stopped.

Her mother didn't notice, anyway. As she scooped pancakes off the griddle and onto a plate, Mrs. Oleson spread a thin layer of melting butter on each one.

Finally breakfast was ready. Mrs. Oleson spread a fresh white cloth over the table in the parlor. Nellie and Willie put out clean china plates and tall glasses and shiny silver forks. Mrs. Oleson put the pancakes on a sky-blue platter in the center of the table. She sent Nellie into the store to get a bottle of golden maple syrup that had come all the way from New England on the train.

They all sat around the square table. "Let us give thanks," Mr. Oleson said, bowing his head.

As he said grace, Nellie thought about the boxes that were piled below the stockings. She wondered which ones were for her and what was in them. She wondered if any exciting presents had made it through the snow on the train from back east. But most of all she thought about how the best present in the entire world would be her father telling them they were all going back to New York.

THE MOST BEAUTIFUL DOLL

At last, after all the breakfast dishes were cleaned away and the parlor was tidy, it was time for the Olesons to open their presents. Nellie got lots and lots of presents. She got a book of Mother Goose rhymes with shiny pictures on every page. She got a new boughten dress for the summertime made of white lawn with blue flowers. She got new hair ribbons, sunrise pink and china blue and lacy white. She got a new cloak of deep-blue wool with black embroidery along the edges to wear to church on Sundays in the winter. She got a new set of pretty clothes for her doll, Laura.

One box she opened held a wooden circle the size of an embroidery hoop and four wooden sticks as long as her forearms. Sunny yellow ribbons were tied to the hoop.

"This is a game called graces," her mother explained. "I played it all the time when I was a child." She picked up two of the sticks and looped the hoop over them. She showed Nellie how to lift the hoop on the sticks and fling it up in the air. "Then the other girl tries to catch the hoop on her sticks. You throw it back and forth until one of you drops it."

"I can do that!" Nellie said. She picked up the other two sticks. "Throw it to me!"

"Not right now, Nellie," Mrs. Oleson said. "Perhaps later. Or you can play it with one of your friends." She turned to one of her presents from Mr. Oleson.

Nellie turned the hoop over in her hands. She wondered who she could play graces with. Maybe Christy Kennedy. Nellie almost never invited other little girls to her house. But she wanted to try the game. And Christy was nicer than some of the other girls, even if she was so much poorer than Nellie.

Willie was very surprised when he opened the nutcracker.

"Say thank you to your sister," Mrs. Oleson said.

"Yah, yah, yah!" Willie said, making the nutcracker's mouth open and shut. Nellie thought he was yanking on the lever too hard. She was afraid the wood would crack and break off in his hand.

Willie made the nutcracker march across the floor. He made the nutcracker stamp all over his armies of tin soldiers. Then he took a piece of pancake and stuffed it in the nutcracker's mouth.

"Yum yum," Willie said, moving the mouth up and down so it looked like the nutcracker was chewing.

"Willie, no!" Nellie said in dismay. Bits of pancake were getting stuck in the nutcracker's soft white beard. Mashed pancake filled the nutcracker's mouth and made it sticky. Now instead of going *clack clack* when his mouth opened and closed, the nutcracker made a smooshing mushy sound. Willie had ruined the nutcracker in the first five minutes of playing with it.

"Willie, stop making a mess," Mrs. Oleson said. "Here, Nellie, open this present."

Her mother handed her a long white box. Nellie lifted the lid carefully.

Inside was the most beautiful doll Nellie had ever seen. Her head was resting on a tiny blue satin pillow, and she was surrounded by folds of silk-thin white paper. Like Nellie, she had shining golden hair in perfect curls. Her skin was soft and tinged with pink, so she looked alive. Her eyes were closed, and soft golden eyelashes brushed her rosy cheeks.

She was even more beautiful than Nellie's china doll, Laura.

"How does she look so alive?" Nellie asked, touching the doll's face.

"She is made of wax, not china," said her mother.

Willie scrambled over to look. "Wax?" he said. "Like a candle? You mean it would melt if we set it on fire?"

Nellie snatched the doll out of the box and held her away from him. "You will do no such thing, Willie Oleson!" she snapped. As she lifted up the doll, her wide blue eyes opened, and they looked just like Nellie's pretty blue eyes. The doll reached out her arms and said, "Mamma!"

"Let me see it," Willie said, holding out his sticky, syrup-covered hands.

"No!" Nellie yelled. "She's mine!" She hugged the doll closer, and again the doll said, "Mamma!" Nellie had never heard of a talking doll before. This doll was magical. She would never let Willie anywhere near her.

"Stop shouting," Mr. Oleson said, lowering his book to glare at them. "Some of us are trying to have a peaceful holiday."

"Nellie won't share!" Willie cried.

"Nellie, let your brother see the doll," Mrs. Oleson said.

"I won't!" Nellie said. "He'll break her like he breaks everything!"

"Willie, don't break Nellie's doll," Mrs. Oleson said wearily.

"I *woooooooon't*," Willie whined. "I just want to *seeeeeee* it."

"No, no, no!" Nellie shouted. She clutched her doll to her chest and stamped into the bedroom.

"Mamma!" cried the doll. "Mamma!"

Nellie sat down on the bed and looked at the doll all over. She had tiny little fingernails. Between her little lips two small white teeth were visible, as if the doll was about to smile. And her dress must be the most beautiful dress in the world. It was made of blue silk, and it draped all the way down to the doll's tiny feet. Nellie wished she had a long dress of blue silk. If this doll were a real lady, she could go to any elegant party that she wanted to.

Nellie took off the doll's dress to see what was underneath. Real petticoats! And much fancier petticoats than Nellie wore. These were trimmed with lace and had lots of ruffles to make the skirt of the dress look fuller. Underneath them were real silky white drawers that Nellie could take off. And on her feet were blue leather slippers that also came off.

Nellie had undressed her doll completely. Now she could put all her clothes back on, stopping to feel how soft each bit of clothing was. But first the doll lay on the bed with her eyes closed, looking peaceful. Nellie lifted her up, and the doll's eyes opened again. "Mamma!" she cried, lifting her hands.

"What is your name?" Nellie said to the doll. She squeezed the doll's stomach.

"Mamma!" said the doll.

"No, silly," Nellie said. "*I'm* your mamma. What's *your* name?"

"Mamma!" said the doll again. Nellie laughed.

"You look just like me," Nellie said. "You are beautiful and elegant with golden curls and blue eyes, like me. Perhaps I will call you Nellie."

Suddenly the doll was whisked out of her hands.

"That's stupid," Willie said, holding the doll over his head.

"Willie!" Nellie yelled at the top of her lungs. "GIVE HER BACK!"

She lunged at Willie, but he darted out of reach, laughing. He ran around the bed with Nellie chasing him. She tripped over the rug and fell into the dresser, knocking over some of her mother's perfumes.

"Keep it quiet in there!" Mr. Oleson called.

"Is this Nellie Junior?" Willie taunted, climbing on the bed. "Does she scream the same way when I pull her hair?" He yanked on one of the doll's beautiful curls.

"Mamma!" the doll cried.

"Willie Oleson, you will be sorry for this!" Nellie said. She grabbed his legs and pulled them out from under him so he fell over on the bed. He landed on top of the doll and scrambled away to the other side.

"What happens when I punch her?" he said. He made a fist and punched the doll in the stomach as hard as he could.

"Mamma!" the poor doll cried again.

"If you don't give her back, I'm going to break all your toys!" Nellie said. She ran back out into the parlor. Mrs. Oleson was preparing the kitchen for dinner. Mr. Oleson was smoking his pipe, so the whole room smelled like tobacco smoke.

Nellie ran over to Willie's tin soldiers and began stamping on them. She grabbed one of the books he'd been given, a Bible story about Joseph's coat of many colors, and she tore out some of the pages, then threw it back down on the floor. She kicked his velocipede until it fell over. She was so mad, she couldn't stop herself.

"Nellie!" her mother said in a horrified voice. Willie came running out of the bedroom, still holding her doll. His mouth dropped open.

Nellie picked up the nutcracker. She grabbed the lever on the back and yanked it up so hard that it snapped off in her hand. She ripped out tufts of the nutcracker's hair, and then she threw it against the wall.

"Stop it!" Willie yelled. He dropped her doll and ran to his velocipede. Quickly, Nellie darted over and snatched up her doll. But as she stood up, she found her mother standing over her with a furious expression on her face.

"Danielle Genevieve Oleson!" Mrs. Oleson

said. "I have never seen anything so unladylike and undignified and wasteful and disrespectful in all my days! Do you know how much that book cost? Or that nutcracker?"

"I don't care!" Nellie said. "Willie deserved it!"

"Your father and I work hard to buy you nice things," Mrs. Oleson said. "Until you learn the value of your presents, you won't be playing with them at all." She took the doll out of Nellie's hands and marched into the bedroom. Nellie followed her.

"But she's mine!" Nellie said. "Willie took her! He's the bad one! Punish him, not me!"

Mrs. Oleson gathered up the doll's clothes and put them back on her, neatly tucking everything into place. Then she carried the doll into the parlor, put her back in her box, set the lid on top, and placed the box in the bottom drawer of the largest dresser.

"Mother!" Nellie wailed. "I want to play with my doll! It's Willie's fault! He started it!"

"We will not discuss this any further," Mrs. Oleson said. She pulled one of the wooden chairs out from the table and set it against the wall. "You will sit quietly in this chair until dinner, and then again from dinner until supper, and you will not talk, you will not scream and fuss, you will not do anything but sit still until you have proven to me that you can be a proper young lady."

"But—" Nellie said.

"Sit!" Mrs. Oleson barked.

Nellie sat on the chair. She wrapped her feet around the round wooden legs. She crossed her arms and slumped. She scowled.

Mrs. Oleson picked up the pages of the torn book. She picked up the pieces of the nutcracker. She set them down on the table and went into the store.

Mr. Oleson hadn't moved from his rocking chair. He puffed on his pipe and frowned at Nellie. Then he picked up a catalogue and began flipping through it.

Across the room, Willie was organizing his tin soldiers into neat rows in their box. He caught her looking at him and stuck his tongue out at her.

The pale china clock on the mantelpiece

ticked and ticked. Everything was very quiet.

Mrs. Oleson came back into the parlor with a bottle of glue and a small brush. She sat down at the table and began to glue the nutcracker back together. She did not look over at Nellie.

Nobody looked at Nellie for a long time. Even Willie was quiet and good. They had never seen Mrs. Oleson so angry. Nellie knew that Willie did not want to get yelled at the way Nellie had.

It wasn't fair. He had started it. He had stolen her doll. Willie should be the one sitting in the chair, not her. Nellie slouched lower and kicked her feet.

She couldn't wait for Christmas to be over.

Laura Ingalls

It was a mild winter, but Nellie hated it anyway. Soon after Christmas an icy-cold rain blew in and washed away all the snow. It rained for days and days. The streets in town were muddy swamps, and it seemed as if every bit of that mud got tracked into the store and scraped all over the floor. Nellie got soaked to the bone every time she stepped outside—when she went to the pump for water, when she walked to Sunday school, when she was sent to look for letters at the post office. She felt like she spent half of the winter standing by the stove, shivering and dripping and trying to warm up, with her flat wet hair plastered to her head instead of shining and curly as it should be.

Finally the spring came, and it was time for school once again. Nellie was almost pleased. At last she could get out of her boring house and away from all her mother's boring chores.

Also, Nellie had a plan. She had read a story in *Youth Magazine* about two girls her age who were best friends. She liked the sound of that—"best friend." She could be somebody's best friend. She was the best at many things: at being pretty, at being rich, at being popular. She liked the idea that someone might think she was the best of all her friends.

She had chosen Christy Kennedy to be her best friend. Maud was too dull, and Becky was too quiet, and Rosemary had a loud, tinny laugh. There weren't a lot of choices in a town as small as Walnut Grove. Christy Kennedy would have to do.

Her plan seemed to go all right for the first week of school. Christy had forgotten about being mad at Nellie before Christmas. Nellie waited for her in the street sometimes so they could walk to school together. They walked home together at dinnertime. They sat on the same bench, and sometimes Nellie drew pictures on her slate to make Christy laugh. At recess they played games with the other girls. Christy said that her favorite game was ring-around-a-rosy, so Nellie decided it was her favorite, too.

Then everything changed.

Nellie did not know when she woke up that Monday morning that everything was about to go horribly wrong. She was feeling happier than usual. All Sunday she had played with her beautiful wax doll, whom she'd named Guinevere. A box of colorful candy had come in on the last train, with some new kinds that Nellie had never seen before. And the sunny spring weather was the only kind of prairie weather that Nellie could tolerate. It was no longer cold and not yet too hot. It was much easier to be pretty in this kind of weather.

Nellie decided to wear the white lawn dress that she had gotten for Christmas. Her mother brushed her hair into long curls and tied two big ribbon bows on top, blue to match the flowers of the dress. Nellie laced up her shoes, feeling pleased that her feet would not be dirty at the end of the day. Christy's feet were always dusty because she went barefoot in the spring.

Outside, Christy and Sandy were waiting on the steps. Willie and Sandy ran on ahead as Nellie and Christy walked down the path to the schoolhouse.

"What a pretty dress, Nellie," Christy said. Christy was wearing the same green calico dress she wore most days.

"Yes, it is," Nellie said. "Of course it is not my prettiest dress, but I like how the blue flowers match my eyes."

"Ma is reading us the most wonderful book," Christy said. She could leap from subject to subject like a grasshopper. Nellie thought this was very irritating. "It's called *Little Women*," Christy said, "and it's all about a family with four daughters, and I think if I could be any of them I would want to be Jo because she is funny, but perhaps I ought to want to be Beth because she is so good."

"It sounds boring," Nellie said. She didn't like it when Christy talked about things Nellie didn't know about. Nellie hadn't even heard of the book, so why would she care which character Christy might be?

"It's not at all boring!" Christy said. "They are a very interesting family."

"Are they rich?" Nellie asked.

"No, I don't think so," Christy said.

"Then *I* wouldn't find them interesting," Nellie said.

"Oh, Nellie, must you be so stuck-up?" Christy said.

"I would rather be stuck-up than a pauper and a nobody," Nellie huffed. She flounced away from Christy and over to the steps of the school. Once she was in the shade, she carefully lowered her sunbonnet and smoothed her dress. Then she sat on the steps to wait for school to begin.

Christy ran over to Maud and the other girls. Soon Nellie could hear her talking about the book again. She crossed her ankles in what she hoped was a ladylike fashion. She watched the boys running back and forth in front of the schoolhouse, calling to one another. Their voices carried across the wide prairie.

Suddenly she saw something new.

Two girls were walking up the long path from town. Nellie had never seen them before.

The taller one had long blond hair, almost as pale gold as Nellie's, tied into two tight braids. The other girl looked to be Nellie's age, and she had thick brown hair, also in braids. They both wore sunbonnets and calico dresses that were too short for them, with their long bare legs and bare feet sticking out below. The older girl was carrying a stack of three books, and the younger held a tin dinner pail.

Nellie instantly knew she would not like them. They must live on a claim far outside town, which was why they had never come to school before. She could tell by how short their dresses were that they were poor. Furthermore, the older one was much too pretty, and the younger was not pretty enough. As they came closer, everyone stopped their games and turned to look at the newcomers.

Suddenly the brown-haired girl called out, "You all sounded just like a flock of prairie chickens!" The blond girl's cheeks turned scarlet, but her sister looked defiant and bold.

Nellie couldn't believe anyone would speak like that to a school yard full of children she'd never met. Had she never been taught any manners?

"Snipes, yourselves!" Sandy Kennedy shouted back. "Snipes! Snipes! Long-legged snipes!"

Willie immediately took up the cry. "Snipes!" he hollered. "Yah, yah! Bare-legged chickens!"

Christy Kennedy stomped up to Sandy and shoved him. "Shut up, Sandy!" she said. All the boys quieted down. Christy went up to the younger new girl. Nellie heard her ask her name.

"I'm Laura Ingalls," said the girl.

Laura Ingalls, Nellie thought. She remembered Charles Ingalls, the man who had first come into the store almost a year ago. These must be the daughters he had mentioned when he came into the store with his wife.

She narrowed her eyes. She didn't like the look of this Laura Ingalls. She especially didn't like the way Christy was smiling and chattering away at her. Almost at once the two of them were talking like they were old friends. Nellie stood up and came slowly down the steps toward them.

As she walked closer, she heard Christy say, "Beadle's store and post office, before you get to the blacksmith shop. Miss Eva Beadle's our teacher." Nellie wondered why Christy hadn't mentioned the Olesons' store as well. Christy noticed her standing there and said, "That's Nellie Oleson," to Laura.

Laura gave Nellie a wide, friendly smile. Nellie didn't know why Christy was being so nice to this stranger. These Ingalls girls were nobody special. Nellie looked Laura up and down, the way she had seen her mother do. She looked over at Laura's sister. She wrinkled up her nose.

"Hm!" she said. "Country girls!" That should show Christy exactly what Nellie thought of her new friend.

To Nellie's surprise, Laura didn't look ashamed. She looked mad.

Just then Teacher rang the bell. Nellie swung around and flounced into the schoolhouse. Behind her Teacher was welcoming the Ingalls girls. As she slid onto her bench, Laura and her sister went up to the front platform with Teacher. Nellie heard Laura's sister say that her name was Mary. Laura was nearly eight, almost as old as Nellie, and Mary was nine.

Nellie was pleased to hear that Laura could not read and did not know the whole alphabet. Nellie was not only prettier and richer than Laura Ingalls, she must be smarter as well.

But one thing Laura clearly could do was be good. She sat quietly on her bench the rest of the morning, studying in one of the books the girls had brought. She read from the front while Mary studied the later pages. Nellie was surprised to see how well behaved they were. After the way Laura had called out on the playground, Nellie had hoped she would be one of those mischievous, naughty girls. Nellie would have liked to see someone else get in trouble.

At recess Christy pulled Laura over to the other little girls, while Mary Ingalls went to sit with Cassie Kennedy.

"Do you all live in town?" Laura asked them.

"Most of us," Christy answered. "Becky's family has a claim about a mile that way."

"So I have to walk here in the morning, too," Becky said. "How far do you have to go?"

"Pa says Plum Creek is two and a half miles from town," Laura said.

"Two and a half miles!" Nellie said snootily. "I am glad *I* don't live in the country. I would hate to walk that far every day. Why, I would need new shoes every other week!" She tossed her curls back. "And if we lived in the country, we probably couldn't even afford them. I am so glad my father is a storekeeper and not a poor farmer."

"I don't mind the walk," Laura said. "It is much prettier out on the prairie, especially in the morning with the sun shining and the rabbits hopping about."

"I'm sure you're right," Christy said. "It can be so dusty and horrid in town sometimes. I'd rather live out in the fresh clean air, like you."

Nellie scowled. Why would Christy want to be like this country girl, Laura, instead of her? She grabbed Christy's hand.

"Let's play ring-around-a-rosy!" she declared.

"Oh, let's!" cried Laura, taking Christy's other hand. "Becky, you be in the middle."

Nellie was shocked. *She* always chose who went in the middle. Who did Laura Ingalls think she was? But the other girls were already joining hands around Becky. Nellie couldn't change it without making a big fuss. It would be better to watch and wait to see what else Laura did.

Still, she was definitely right about one thing. She did not like that Laura Ingalls, not one bit.

COUNTRY GIRLS

Nellie was displeased to find out that Laura Ingalls was smarter than she first appeared. By the end of the first day she was reading her letters as if she'd known how to all along. She must have studied at home, Nellie thought.

That night Nellie could not concentrate on her studies. She was distracted during supper, and while she was helping to wash up, her hand slipped in the suds and she dropped a china plate, which shattered on the floor. Mrs. Oleson made her clean it up and then sent her into the bedroom to stay out of the way.

Nellie brought out Guinevere and told her doll about the unsettling new strangers at school.

"Don't you worry, Nellie," she imagined Guinevere saying. "You are still the prettiest girl in school. All the other girls want to be like you. Laura Ingalls is just new. They will get bored with her soon."

The next morning, Nellie wore a pink dress with little pink rose-shaped buttons down the front. She stood in front of the mirror for a long time, making sure each curl was perfect. Today everything would be back to normal, she told herself. They were just country girls.

"Nellie, hurry up!" Willie called.

She picked up her books and slate and rushed through the parlor into the store. As the door banged shut behind her, she realized there were customers at the counter.

It was Laura Ingalls and her sister, Mary.

Nellie wrinkled her nose. What were *they* doing here? She tried to look like she had not been running. She hoped her father would not say anything about chores or dusting in front of the Ingalls girls. She wanted them to know that she was rich and that she could do and have anything she wanted. She wanted Laura especially to know that.

Laura did not look pleased to see Nellie, either. She did not say good morning to her. She acted as if Nellie was not there. Instead she kept gazing around with wide eyes. Nellie saw her looking at the two tall pails of candy.

"Yah! Yah!" Willie pointed at the girls and laughed. "Long-legged snipes!" he cried. Mary turned pink again and looked down at the counter. Laura, on the other hand, lifted her chin and clenched her jaw as if she was thinking about yelling something back. Nellie wished she would. Then Mr. Oleson would know that Mary and Laura were rude country girls.

"Shut up, Willie," Mr. Oleson said, turning to the shelves behind him.

"Snipes! Snipes!" Willie said. He started doing a dance, pulling up his trouser legs and capering about. "Snipes!"

Laura still did not look ashamed. Nellie tossed her curls. She knew how to put Laura in her place. She went over to one of the pails of candy and dug her hands in. She pulled out a wavy ribbon of green-and-white candy and stuck it in her mouth. With her other hand she grabbed a handful of round pink-and-white peppermints. *See,* she thought, looking at Laura, *I can have anything I want. Don't you wish you were like me, country girl?* Willie went over to the other pail and grabbed some candy too.

"Nellie! You and Willie go right back out of here!" Mr. Oleson said. But Nellie knew that he was not really paying attention to them. His mind was on his customers and what he had to sell. He did not care what Nellie and Willie did when customers were in the store.

Mary untied a round silver coin from a handkerchief pinned inside her pocket. She slid the coin across the counter to Mr. Oleson and, in a quiet voice, she asked for a slate.

Of course, Nellie thought. *They had to borrow Teacher's yesterday.* She shoved more of the peppermints into her mouth. Her stomach was starting to feel a little sick from so much candy first thing in the morning. But she would never let Laura know that.

Mr. Oleson handed Mary a slate. "You'll want a slate pencil, too. Here it is. One penny."

Mary hesitated, and Nellie quickly swallowed a round candy ball, which made her throat feel odd and scraped.

"They haven't got a penny," she said fast, before Laura could admit it.

"Well, take it along and tell your Pa to give me the penny next time he comes to town," Mr. Oleson said. Nellie sniffed. Mrs. Oleson hated it when Mr. Oleson sold things on credit. She was afraid he didn't keep track of it well enough. She didn't want them to lose money if any of these poor farmers couldn't pay for the supplies they borrowed. If it were up to Mrs. Oleson, everyone would pay in cash right up front. Nellie agreed with her. Why should they trust poor people to pay them back?

Still, she was surprised when Mary said, "No, sir. Thank you." She turned around and walked out of the store with Laura behind her. As she pushed open the screen door, Laura turned around and gave Nellie a hard look, like she was trying to figure her out. Nellie didn't like it. Laura acted very superior for a poor country girl.

Nellie made a face and stuck out her tongue. Laura finally looked startled. She hurried outside, the screen door banging behind her.

Ha, Nellie thought. *Take that, Laura Ingalls.*

She wondered why Mary had said no to the slate pencil. Was it because she knew the Ingallses couldn't afford it? Or maybe she didn't want to be beholden to the Olesons. Nellie was offended. She didn't want to give store credit, but if her father offered it, the least they could do was accept it. They should show more gratitude. Her father was being very generous, in Nellie's opinion.

Well, I don't care, Nellie thought. *They'll just have to come back in here tomorrow to buy the pencil. And then Laura will see me eat even more candy and she'll be even more jealous. Ha!*

She dropped her last handful of candy back into the pail and followed Willie to the door. Her hands felt sticky and her throat was still raw from swallowing the candy ball too fast. Also, her stomach was queasy, and it was all Laura's fault.

Outside, Sandy was waiting for Willie, but Christy Kennedy wasn't there. Nellie looked down the street toward Christy's house. She didn't see her coming. She looked in the other direction, toward the schoolhouse. She could see Laura and Mary walking down the path through the grass, but she couldn't see Christy.

At least Christy wasn't with Laura. Perhaps she had simply forgotten to wait for Nellie.

When Nellie got to school, Christy was already sitting on her bench. Laura was standing next to her, and they were chattering away like magpies. Laura said something and Christy laughed. Then Teacher called them all to attention, and Laura had to go sit next to Mary.

Nellie slid onto the bench beside Christy. She waited until Teacher's attention was distracted, going over spelling words with Laura. Then Nellie leaned over and whispered hello to Christy.

"Good morning, Nellie," Christy whispered

back. "Goodness, isn't the wind strong today? I had to clutch my sunbonnet to my head all the way here. I thought it might pick me up and blow me out of town and all the way to Plum Creek. That's where Laura lives. It sounds so pretty," she said.

"I'm certain it isn't," Nellie said. "My father says the Ingallses live in a hole in the *ground*. Imagine! He says their walls are made of dirt and the ceiling is grass and they live right in the side of a mudbank." She shuddered. Surely Christy wouldn't want to be friends with Laura if she knew the whole truth about her.

"Oh, I know!" Christy said. "Laura told me all about it. It sounds so exciting! Nothing like our ordinary boring houses."

"It doesn't sound exciting, it sounds *dirty*," Nellie said. "There must be earthworms crawling through the walls right beside their heads. I bet their clothes and hair are full of bugs and dirt and they don't even know it."

"I'm sure that's not true," Christy said, sounding shocked. "Besides, they don't live there anymore. Laura's pa built them a big beautiful house with glass windows and an attic. She says it's full of light and air. I can't wait to see it!"

"Why would you ever see it?" Nellie said. "It's miles and miles away."

"I know," Christy said. "But now that Laura and I are friends, maybe one day she'll invite me out for a visit." She beamed happily, and Nellie felt like a knife was twisting in her stomach. Perhaps it was still the candy making her feel ill, she thought.

"Christy," Nellie said in a low voice, "I don't think your parents would want you to be friends with someone like Laura."

"What do you mean?" Christy asked.

"You don't know anything about them," Nellie whispered. "They've never come to Sunday school, and Father says they had to abandon their last claim. And I saw Laura and Mary in the store this morning buying a slate. They don't even have enough money to afford a slate pencil. That's how poor they are, Christy."

"Nellie Oleson," Christy said with a frown, "you should stop spreading such terrible stories.

I'm sure the Ingallses are very good people. Laura and Mary are nice, and I am glad they're here."

She turned her back on Nellie and stuck her nose in her reader.

"But—" Nellie protested. "But I'm only telling the truth."

"Shhhh," Christy said, loud enough to make Teacher look up. Her expression was stern, and Nellie knew she couldn't talk anymore.

Her insides felt like they were burning up. Why wouldn't Christy listen to her? Nellie had been her friend much longer than this penniless country girl. Christy shouldn't be defending *Laura* when she'd known her for only a day. It wasn't fair and it wasn't right.

Nellie was mad the whole rest of the day. She was mad during recess, even though the other girls agreed when she insisted on playing ring-around-a-rosy again. She was mad when she went home for dinner, kicking the table legs with such force that her mother looked up from her chicken pie to reprimand her sternly. And she was mad that evening as she sat in the parlor with her book open on the table.

The only thing that would make her feel better, she was sure, would be showing off in front of Laura again the next day.

But when the next morning came, Mary and Laura did not appear in Mr. Oleson's store. Nellie woke up early and dressed in a hurry. She made sure she looked perfect, and then she flounced into the store to wait for the Ingalls sisters. She sat on a barrel beside the counter and chose a piece of candy to begin with, although she did not eat it yet. She did not want to feel as sick as she had the day before. She had to save the candy until Laura came in to buy her slate pencil.

"Nellie, what are you doing?" her father asked. He was using a knife to cut open a box on the counter.

"Nothing," Nellie said. "Waiting. What is that?"

"Sewing supplies," Mr. Oleson said. He opened the box, and Nellie could see a stack of silver thimbles. Spools of colorful thread were packed around the edges, black and red and bright yellow. In between were coils of shiny ribbons and lace and a few balls of thick woolen yarn for knitting.

"Oh," Nellie said, disappointed. She had hoped it would be more candy, or perhaps a new toy from back east that she could play with in front of Laura.

Mr. Oleson did not say anything more. He was busy writing down an inventory of all the supplies in the box. As he wrote each item down, he took it out and stacked it on the counter beside him. He worked quickly and was not very careful about what he was doing. Nellie noticed that he had written down seven thimbles when there were really eight. But she didn't say anything. Her father did not like to be corrected.

Nobody came into the store. The clock on the top shelf ticked closer and closer to schooltime. Nellie got up off the barrel and wandered over to the front window. Dust whirled down the street outside in puffs like smoke.

Suddenly Nellie saw a movement across the street at Mr. Beadle's store. The door opened, and Laura and Mary came out! They stopped on the front steps for a moment, and Nellie could see that Laura was holding a new slate pencil in her hand.

Nellie was furious. They had deliberately gone to Mr. Beadle's store for their pencil instead of Mr. Oleson's. Why would they do that? Wasn't her father's store good enough for them?

Then she saw Teacher come out the door behind them. Laura and Mary smiled up at her and she smiled back. Together they walked down the steps and along the street toward the schoolhouse. Laura swung her dinner pail and talked, and Teacher nodded and said something back to her. They looked very friendly. Nellie had never walked to school with Teacher. She had never even thought of doing it.

Perhaps Laura wanted to be the "teacher's pet." Perhaps she was deliberately buying things at Mr. Beadle's store to make friends with Teacher. Perhaps she thought if she smiled and was sweet to her, Teacher would be nicer to her in school. Laura didn't know that Teacher was nice to everyone. Although Nellie could not remember Teacher smiling at *her* like that. Certainly not since the day of the bugs in her desk.

Nellie felt mad and sick all over again. She couldn't even eat her candy, although she stuck it in her pocket to eat at recess. At least she could do it in front of Laura then.

But it made her so angry. How dare Laura Ingalls decide that Mr. Oleson's store wasn't good enough for her? How dare she try to become Teacher's favorite? What nasty trick would she try next?

Scheming, stuck-up country girls!

School Yard Games

The long spring days dragged on, getting hotter and hotter. Nellie hated school more than ever, now that she had to see Laura Ingalls every day. Christy and Laura had quickly become fast friends. Nellie guessed they would even call themselves "best friends." It was as if Christy had never thought of Nellie that way at all.

Nellie tried not to care. She told herself that Christy wasn't good enough to be her best friend anyhow. Christy's family was not as rich as hers, and they had too many children, and

Christy talked too much, on and on about things nobody cared about, least of all Nellie. She was better off without her.

Laura had passed Nellie in her studies after only a couple of weeks. Nellie did not know how she'd done it. Laura must spend all her time at home studying. She couldn't possibly have any good toys to play with if she had so much time to spend with her books. It made Nellie mad to see how pleased Teacher was with Laura.

On Fridays especially, when Laura spelled more words right than Nellie, Nellie felt so mad that she wanted to grab her slate and break it over Laura's head. Only knowing how much trouble she would be in with Teacher stopped her. She did not want Laura to have the satisfaction of watching Nellie get punished. Laura never got into trouble. Nellie could imagine the smug look on Laura's face if Teacher ever used her ruler on Nellie.

At least Nellie was still queen of the school yard. She made the other girls play ring-around-a-rosy every day. She liked to hear them all singing and watch them circle around her as if she was the center of the universe. She liked the way they all fell down together in a big pile as if they were all friends. She wondered if Christy remembered telling Nellie that this was her favorite game, and if she knew that Nellie made them play it for that reason.

One Friday at recess Nellie came out of the schoolhouse to find Laura winding a chain of wildflowers around Christy's wrist. The flowers were yellow and blue and white, like the sky, and Christy was laughing.

Then Laura turned and looked directly at Nellie. She said in a loud voice, "Let's play Uncle John!"

Nellie didn't know why, but she felt afraid. She felt as if she was standing on the edge of the prairie with a tornado rushing toward her. Nobody had ever challenged Nellie at recess before.

"Let's! Let's!" cried Rosemary and Maud and the other girls. They sounded so excited. Nellie felt betrayed.

Then Christy took Laura's hand and said,

"Yes, let's play Uncle John!" And that was the worst betrayal of all. Hadn't Nellie picked ring-around-a-rosy because it was Christy's favorite? Wasn't *she* supposed to be Christy's best friend? What did this stuck-up, barefoot country girl have that Nellie didn't?

Her mad feelings boiled over until she could hardly see. Her skin felt like it was going to burst into flames. Nellie clenched her fists, and then she grabbed Laura's long thick braids and yanked as hard as she could, jerking Laura to the ground.

"No! No!" Nellie yelled. "I want to play ring-around-a-rosy!"

The other girls froze. Maud pressed her hands to her face. Christy's mouth was a wide "O." Becky's eyes looked as big as pancakes. There was a hushed silence. Nellie stood over Laura and felt strong and proud for the first time in weeks.

Laura jumped quickly to her feet. Her face looked as mad as Nellie felt. She lifted her hand, and for a moment, Nellie thought Laura was going to slap her. She knew what she would do if that happened. She would pull

Laura's hair again, and then she would kick her shins, and then she would bite her arm and scratch her face, and she didn't care who saw or how much trouble she got in. She just wanted to hurt Laura the way she'd been hurt.

But Laura stopped herself. She did not slap Nellie. She lowered her hand and held it in a fist, breathing heavily. She stared right into Nellie's eyes. Nellie wondered what Laura was thinking with such a defiant face. Laura seemed like someone from out of a storybook, not like a real little girl who had feelings like Nellie.

"Come on, Laura," Christy said gently. She took one of Laura's hands, and Maud took the other. The rest of the girls joined hands around Nellie, and they all began to go in a circle.

Nellie breathed a sigh of relief. She'd won! She was still in charge, not Laura Ingalls. No matter how much Christy liked her, Laura was no match for Nellie.

Then Christy started to sing:

"Uncle John is sick abed.
What shall we send him?"

The other girls chimed in. All of them! Every single one chose to side with Laura instead of her!

"No! No!" Nellie screamed. "Ring-around-a-rosy! Or I won't play!" She ran at Laura's and Christy's hands and broke them apart. The circle of girls backed away from her. None of them looked sorry. None of them stuck up for her. They'd known her for years and they just stood there staring at her. Nellie could feel tears welling up behind her eyes. She turned and ran all the way through the grass and up the steps and into the schoolhouse.

Behind her, as she ran away, she heard Christy say, "All right, you get in the middle, Maud."

The schoolhouse was empty. All the children were outside playing. The sound of the boys shouting drifted through the open window on one side. On the other side, the girls were singing the Uncle John song. Nellie heard them all yell together, "By Laura Ingalls!" which meant Laura would go into the middle of the ring.

Nellie sat down on a bench, put her head on her arms, and sobbed. She cried and cried and cried, and she still felt as if she had more tears piling up inside her.

It didn't matter that she was the prettiest and the richest. All those girls liked Laura Ingalls instead, and Nellie could not understand why.

Not a single girl followed her into the schoolhouse. Nobody came to make sure she was all right. Nobody came to ask her to come back and play with them. Nobody wanted her to come back. Nobody cared that she was crying. Nobody wanted to be her friend at all.

Laura Ingalls had ruined everything.

After a long while, Nellie's sobs turned into hiccups and gasps. She sniffled and tried to catch her breath.

Then she felt a hand on her shoulder. Someone had come for her! Someone did care about her after all.

She lifted her head, hoping to see Christy. But to her surprise, the gentle face of Teacher was looking down at her.

"Nellie, what's wrong?" Teacher asked.

Nellie tried to wipe her face with her hands. She didn't like having Teacher see her this way. Part of her didn't want anyone else to know what had happened outside.

Teacher reached into one of her pockets and pulled out a white linen handkerchief embroidered with tiny yellow daisies. She passed the handkerchief to Nellie and sat down on the bench in front of hers, her elbows resting on the back of the seat.

Nellie dried her eyes and blew her nose. She took a deep breath and felt a tiny bit calmer.

"What happened?" Teacher asked.

"Th-the other girls don't like me," Nellie sniffled. "They l-l-like L-Laura better than m-me. Nobody w-wants to be my friend anymore."

"Nellie," Teacher said, "have you thought about what it means to be someone's friend?"

"Of c-course," Nellie said. "It means they like you and play with you and don't ever fight with you and you w-walk to school t-together and p-play your favorite g-games at recess . . ." She broke off, feeling tears pricking at her eyes again.

"Some of that is true," said Teacher, "but it's more than that. Sometimes friends *do* fight. They don't always like all the same things. But if they're good friends, they'll find a way to forgive each other. You have to listen and think about what the other girl is feeling. If you want people to be your friend, you have to be a friend to them, too."

"But I am!" Nellie said indignantly. "I gave Christy a piece of my candy last week." She wiped away an angry tear. "But now she's being so mean to me. Her and Laura both. I hate them."

"Hate is a very strong feeling, Nellie," Teacher said. Nellie thought that was true. What she was feeling was very, very strong. Teacher went on, "If you hold on to that hate, it will make you angry and bitter. You can only be happy again if you let go of that feeling and try to see things from another point of view."

"I don't want to," Nellie said sulkily. "They're wrong and they're mean and I don't want to be their friend anyway. I wish I could go back to New York and leave this horrid old town forever."

Teacher sighed. "I have to ring the bell to bring everyone back in." She stood up and looked down at Nellie, hesitating. "Just think about what I've said. Everyone sees things their own way. Maybe if you understood how Laura and Christy felt, you wouldn't be so angry with them."

Nellie was pretty sure she would still be angry. She was sure they were out there laughing at her, pleased about the terrible trick they'd played on her and how they'd made everyone else turn on her, too.

"You can keep the handkerchief," Teacher said with a smile. "And Nellie, if you ever want to talk, I can make time to listen." She went to the schoolhouse door and picked up the bell to ring everyone back in.

Nellie looked down at the crumpled wet fabric in her hands. She didn't need Teacher's handmade handkerchief with its crooked flowers. She had pretty lace boughten handkerchiefs of her own back at home. But she smoothed out the wrinkles, folded it up, and stuck it in her pocket. She could save it to remind herself that not everyone hated her like Laura and Christy did.

Willie was one of the first ones into the schoolhouse. As he passed her bench, he squinted at his sister. "You look terrible," he said. "Your face is all splotchy and pink."

"Shut up, Willie," Nellie snapped.

When Christy came up, Nellie refused to slide over, so she went to sit by Laura instead. But as she walked away, Nellie hissed, "I'm *never* going to speak to you again, Christy Kennedy. You or Laura Ingalls. Never ever ever ever *ever*."

Christy looked a little bit sorry then, but Laura didn't. She just took Christy's hand and tugged her away.

"I don't care," Nellie whispered to herself. "I don't care, I don't, I don't."

Mrs. Oleson's Idea

Nellie was glad that it was Friday and she
did not have to go back to school for two
whole days. Of course, she didn't think anything was going to be better on Monday either.
Maybe she could pretend to be sick. Maybe she
could pretend to be so sick that she would
never have to go back to school.

When she got home, Nellie spent the rest of
the day lying on the parlor rug and staring at
the painting of the Hudson River. She wished
and wished with all her might that she could
go there right this minute.

Nellie's mother didn't usually ask Nellie or Willie about school. She didn't have time to talk to them in the afternoons. But today she came into the parlor shortly before suppertime and saw Nellie lying on the carpet.

"Nellie, what in the name of Heaven are you doing?" Mrs. Oleson asked. "Does that seem like a ladylike posture to you?"

"Nellie is sulking," Willie said with relish from the corner where he was playing with his soldiers. "She was a big baby today. She cried all the way through recess."

"Oh, my," Mrs. Oleson said. "Nellie, I hope you had your handkerchief with you."

"Teacher lent me one," Nellie mumbled.

"Sit up and let me fix your hair," Mrs. Oleson said. She sat down on one of the wooden chairs. Nellie sat on her heels in front of her, and Mrs. Oleson smoothed out the curls Nellie had squashed by lying on the floor. Her hands felt strong and capable, like they could fix any problem, not just messy ringlets.

"Now," her mother said, "tell me what you were crying about."

Before Nellie knew what she was doing, the whole story spilled out. She told her mother all about how Christy was supposed to be her best friend but Laura Ingalls had come along and stolen her. She told how Laura acted proud and superior even though she had no reason to. She told the story of ring-around-a-rosy and Uncle John.

"So now all the girls don't like me," Nellie finished. "And it is all Laura's fault. They used to be my friends until she came along. But nobody wants to be my friend anymore." She blinked fast to stop herself from crying again.

"I'm sure that's not true," Mrs. Oleson said. "Come help me with supper." Nellie trailed along as her mother filled a large iron pot with water and set it on the cookstove. She put six potatoes in the pot, added exactly a teaspoon of salt, and lit the fire to boil the water. Then she turned her attention to the salt pork.

"It is true," Nellie said glumly. "I shall never have any friends ever again."

"Nonsense," her mother said. "You just need to remind them what a special little girl you are. They must have forgotten how much they want to be like you. If you remind them of why they like you, they will want to be your friends again."

"How do I do that?" Nellie asked. "Why do they like me?"

"Because you're the upper class of this town," Mrs. Oleson said. "Your family is wealthy and well-bred, and you must set an example for everyone else by always being gracious and ladylike."

I don't want to be gracious and ladylike, Nellie thought mutinously. *I just want to pull Laura's hair again.*

"I know!" Mrs. Oleson said, clapping her hands together. "We should have a party!"

"A party?" Nellie repeated. She felt a jolt of excitement. "We've never had a party before."

"We used to have them all the time," Mrs. Oleson said. "When I was young, gentlemen vied with each other to take me to parties. There was always dancing and games, and all the girls wore their very best dresses." She sniffed disapprovingly. "Of course, there's not enough society out here in the wilderness for proper parties. And if their best dresses are what they're wearing to church—well!"

"How can we have a party like that?" Nellie said. "None of us know how to dance."

"Oh, you would have a little girls' party," Mrs. Oleson said. "Those are different. Everyone would still have to dress nicely, but we'll play little-girl games. And we can make a cake! We'll use white flour and white sugar from the store. We'll make the nicest cake these country girls have ever seen. Then they'll all be sorry for being so mean to you."

"Will they?" Nellie said, finally feeling happy again. She couldn't wait to see their faces when they realized how sorry they were. They'd remember how rich and fancy Nellie was, and they would all want to be her friends again.

"Absolutely," Mrs. Oleson said. "Everyone wants to know people wealthier than them. I certainly do, but there aren't any here in Walnut Grove."

"Oh, I have the best idea!" Nellie said. "I'll invite all the girls in school *except* Christy and

Laura. That will teach them a lesson! They'll wish they had been nicer so they could have come to my party."

But Mrs. Oleson was shaking her head. "That wouldn't be proper, Nellie. It's good manners to invite all the little girls in your class. Besides, a lady of good breeding does not hold a grudge. She holds herself above her enemies and makes them feel small just through her actions."

My enemies, Nellie thought. *That's what Laura Ingalls is. She is my enemy.*

"But I don't want to invite them." Nellie pouted. "I don't want Laura to have any of my cake."

Mrs. Oleson smiled a little smile. "But just wait until she sees your beautiful house and all your beautiful playthings. Living well is the best revenge, Nellie. Remember that."

Nellie smiled back. "All right, I'll invite them. But I will not be nice to them."

"It's your party," her mother said. "You will be the center of attention and you can do what you like." Nellie liked the sound of that. "How about next Saturday afternoon?" Mrs. Oleson continued.

"I will tell the girls at school on Monday," Nellie said. Her mother gave her a masher and set her to work mashing the soft-boiled potatoes.

Nellie thought about what Teacher had said, about acting like a friend so people would want to be friends with you. Then she thought about her mother's words, about holding herself above her enemies. Maybe she could do both. It was a friendly thing to do, to invite everyone to her party—even Christy and Laura. But it would also make her feel superior and more special than Christy and Laura, because she could have a beautiful town party and they couldn't. So she won both ways. It was a perfect plan.

Nellie thought about the party all weekend. She didn't complain when her mother made her sweep the whole house and dust all the windowsills and shelves and paintings. She wiped down the wooden table and chairs until they shone, and she cleaned the ashes out of the iron stove and polished it. She did everything she was asked, and for once, she tried to do it all the right way as well. She wanted her house to be absolutely perfect for the party. She wanted everyone to see how clean and shiny and refined it was.

Finally Monday came. Nellie wore her white lawn dress to school, and she got there before anyone else. As the other little girls arrived, she stopped each of them and invited them to her party. They were all very surprised. Nellie could tell they had thought she would still be mad about the fight at recess on Friday. They even seemed a little afraid of her at first, like she might pull their hair, too. But she smiled sweetly and she used her politest, most charming voice, and soon they smiled back and said they would love to come.

The only time Nellie's smile slipped was when she saw Christy and Laura walking to school together. They came up the path through the grass arm in arm. Behind them were Mary and Cassie. Christy saw Nellie first and started to slow down, but Laura kept walking like there was nothing wrong, pulling Christy along with her.

Nellie stood on the bottom step. They could not get into the school without passing her. As they came closer, Christy looked more and more nervous. Then Nellie put on her biggest smile, and they both looked confused.

"Hi, girls!" Nellie said. "Isn't it a nice morning?"

"It really is—" Christy started with a relieved expression, but Nellie interrupted her. She didn't want to listen to one of Christy's long rambles right now.

"I just wanted to let you two know that I am having a party at my house next Saturday afternoon. And you two especially *must* come, you *must*. Say you will! I really specially want you both there."

Laura's face was a mix of suspicion and confusion. Nellie was sure she didn't know anything about parties. Christy just looked pleased that Nellie had forgiven her. *Ha,* Nellie thought. *I most certainly have not, Christy Kennedy.*

"Really, a party?" Christy said. "That sounds so wonderful. I've never been to a party. Have you, Laura?"

"N-no," Laura said reluctantly. "I don't know if I can come. I'll have to ask Ma and Pa."

"Of course, your sisters are invited, too," Nellie said. "Mary and Cassie. Surely if Mary comes with you, your parents will let you come to the party, Laura. I mean, you're not a baby, for goodness' sake. If you can walk to town for school, you can do it for my party."

"I will ask them," Laura said. "Thank you for inviting us, Nellie."

Teacher rang the bell for school, and Laura and Christy went up the steps past Nellie. As Nellie followed them, she tried not to frown. There went Laura acting all mannerly and perfect again. It was enough to make Nellie want to scream.

But then Teacher smiled at her. "I heard you inviting the girls to your party, Nellie," Teacher said. "That was very nice of you. I'm glad to see you are trying to be a friend to them."

"Yes, I am," Nellie said. "Just like you told me to." And for the rest of the morning she felt virtuous and proud of herself, and it almost made her understand why Laura wanted to be so good.

The rest of the week went far too slowly for Nellie. She was so impatient for Saturday's party that she could barely concentrate on her studies, and she got almost all the words wrong when Teacher tested her spelling. But Teacher was nicer than ever to Nellie, and the other girls were all so excited about the party that they were nice to Nellie, too. Even Laura said she would come. The party was the only thing any of them could talk about, and it made Nellie feel very important. Her plan was clearly working.

Nellie's mother was excited too. It was as if planning a party made her feel like she was back east again. She had Mr. Oleson rearrange some of the furniture in the parlor to create more space. She washed the white lace curtains so they were freshly starched and fluttered brightly at the windows.

The night before the party, Mrs. Oleson came into the parlor from the store with a wooden box and a secret smile on her face.

"We're going to make something wonderful," she said. "I think none of your friends will ever have had this before."

"What is it?" Nellie asked, standing on tiptoe to peek inside the box.

Mrs. Oleson put the box down on the counter in the kitchen. She lifted out a bright yellow fruit that was round and pockmarked like an orange, but the bright sunny color of buttercups.

"This is a lemon," she said. "Your father got a box of them this week. We're going to use them to make lemonade."

Willie popped up on the other side of Mrs. Oleson. "I want one!" he cried. He grabbed a lemon out of the box and ran to the other side of the parlor.

"Willie!" Mrs. Oleson said. "Give that back right now! Nellie, go get the sack of white sugar from the pantry."

When Nellie came back from the pantry, she saw that Willie had figured out how to peel the skin off his lemon. Mrs. Oleson was choosing a pitcher from the cupboard and ignoring him. Willie stuck out his tongue at Nellie and took a big bite of the lemon.

Instantly his eyes went wide. His face puckered up and his lips got small and wrinkled. "YEEEEEEEUUUUUUUUUUUUUCK!" he yelled, spitting out the bite of lemon into his hand. "That's horrible! That's the worst thing I've ever tasted!" He ran outside to stick his head under the pump and fill his mouth with water.

Nellie turned to her mother anxiously. "Is there something wrong with the lemons?"

To her surprise, her mother was laughing. "It serves him right," Mrs. Oleson said. "Did you see his face?" She laughed so hard, she had to lean over and rest her hands on her knees. Nellie pictured Willie's face again and she started laughing, too. It was a strange, bubbly feeling to be laughing with her mother. Usually her mother was too busy to spend time with her like this. And Nellie had never had anyone to make fun of Willie with her before. She liked the idea that she and her mother were on one side, with dumb, lemon-eating Willie on the other.

"Lemons are sour," her mother finally explained. "You're not supposed to eat them like that. We'll be adding a lot of sugar to the juice, and then it'll be a wonderful drink."

Mrs. Oleson showed Nellie how to roll the lemons on a dish towel on a flat surface to make them juicier. Then she carefully sliced the lemons and squeezed the juice into a tall glass pitcher with a curvy spout and handle. She added water and a cup of sugar, stirring a long wooden spoon around and around the pitcher to make the sugar dissolve. Nellie watched the little bits of lemon, which looked like tiny teardrops and scraps of lace, dance in circles in the pale-yellow liquid. The sugar swirled in the middle like a snowstorm across the prairie.

Mrs. Oleson poured a little into a glass and tasted it. "Hmm," she said. "I think it's still too sour. Here, you try it." She handed the glass to Nellie. Nellie tasted the lemonade and made a face.

"That's what I thought," Mrs. Oleson said. She added several spoonfuls of sugar to the lemonade and stirred it again. Now the taste was sweet and sharp at the same time. Nellie loved it.

"Perfect," her mother said. "Your friends will be so impressed!"

Nellie wished they could stay in the kitchen making lemonade all day, but her mother had inventory and accounting papers to go through with her father that night. So Nellie sat quietly with Guinevere, looking around her beautiful, sparkling-clean house and thinking about what a perfect party it was going to be.

Everyone would be jealous, but everyone would love her. They would see Guinevere and drink the lemonade and wish they could be like Nellie. By the end, they would surely realize that Nellie was a much better friend to have than Laura Ingalls.

And then she would be the most important girl in school once again.

A Very Fancy Party

Nellie woke up early on Saturday. She was tingling all over. A party of her very own! What would everyone think of her house? Would they like the lemonade? Would they break anything? Would Willie be good? There were so many things to think about. But mostly Nellie was just excited. She wished every day could be a party day.

She took a bath and used up nearly an entire piece of soap. Then she put on her prettiest, newest, fanciest dress. The skirt had three layers of ruffles, and there were ruffles at the shoulders and wrists, too. It was the color of dusky pink roses with edges of snowy white lace. It was not as beautiful as Guinevere's dress, but Nellie was sure it was the prettiest dress any little girl in Walnut Grove had ever worn. Under it she wore frilly petticoats edged with lace, and her shoes were newly shined, and even her pink hair ribbons were freshly pressed.

Her mother gave her an apron to wear, and Nellie helped to make the party cake. The best part was the sugar-white frosting. Mrs. Oleson cracked four eggs and separated out the yolks so only the whites of the eggs were left in the bowl. She didn't let Nellie help with this part because it was very important not to mix any yolk in. But she let Nellie bring her the cream of tartar, the powdered sugar, and the rose water.

Nellie leaned on the counter to watch as her mother began to beat the egg whites with a fork. This had to be done very fast and strong, which was why Mrs. Oleson was doing it. Then Nellie measured out the cream of tartar and added it while Mrs. Oleson was still beating. After that she added powdered sugar one tablespoon at a time, waiting while her mother beat it all together. Soon the mixture was a frothy foam, and then it started to look like ocean waves frozen in place, mountains and valleys of white. At the end Nellie added the rose water.

Then Mrs. Oleson got the cake, which had been cooling since she had taken it out of the oven. She sprinkled flour lightly over the whole thing. Then she used a knife to spread the frosting over the top and sides. She did it so smoothly and neatly that it looked like a cake in a picture.

"It's perfect," Nellie said.

"I want some now!" Willie said, but his mother slapped his hand as he reached toward the frosting.

"Don't you touch this cake, Willie Oleson," Mrs. Oleson said, "or I will have your father switch you."

Nellie made a face at Willie. *So there*, she thought. *This is my party, and Mother wants it to be perfect for me.*

Willie stamped around and sulked, but he

didn't go anywhere near the cake for the rest of the morning.

Nellie could barely eat her dinner, she was so excited. As soon as the dishes were cleared, she took off her apron and ran through the store to the front window to see if she could see anyone coming.

Finally she saw four figures approaching from the end of the street. She squinted at them for a moment, then realized it was Laura, Mary, Cassie, and Christy. The Ingalls girls must have stopped to meet up with the Kennedys. Nellie ran back into her parlor and tried to decide where to stand. Should she be sitting when they came in? Should she be at the table? Should she be standing by the door waiting for them? She realized she was clutching a piece of her skirt in each hand.

"Goodness, Nellie, stop being such a whirlwind," Mrs. Oleson said. "You'll wrinkle your dress with all your fussing. Stand still." She stood Nellie in the middle of the room, brushed a few specks of flour off her dress, gave her curls a final pat, and went to the door.

Nellie felt relieved. Her mother had made the decision for her.

Mrs. Oleson opened the door to the store and found the four girls standing there. They were all wearing their best dresses and pretty hair ribbons. But Nellie noticed that none of them were wearing shoes, and Laura's and Mary's feet left dusty footprints on the fine carpet and newly washed floor.

"Good afternoon, Mrs. Oleson," said Mary, and the other three echoed her.

"Good afternoon, girls," Mrs. Oleson said. "Please come in."

"Yes, ma'am," they chorused. Laura's eyes were huge. She kept staring around like she'd never seen carpets or paintings or boughten chairs before. Nellie puffed up with pride.

"Welcome to my party," she said happily. "Be careful not to break anything. I know you never see things this pretty in your own homes."

"Go into the bedroom, girls, and leave your bonnets," Nellie's mother said. They looked around for a minute in confusion until Nellie pointed to the bedroom door.

While they were taking off their bonnets, Becky and Maud and the rest of the girls arrived. Nellie greeted each one and pretended to admire all their dresses, but secretly she kept thinking that hers was the prettiest dress. *The prettiest dress for the prettiest girl.*

Then they were all back in the parlor and staring at Nellie, and for a moment Nellie wondered what she should do. She'd never had a party or been to one before, so she wasn't sure how it was supposed to work. Should she suggest a game? What if she did and Laura made them all play something else instead? She would hate for that to happen at her own party.

Luckily, Mrs. Oleson took charge. She told the girls to sit down, and then she said, "Now, Nellie, bring out your playthings."

Nellie was relieved—now she knew what to do. But she was also worried. What if the girls broke one of her toys? What if Laura did something bad to Nellie's dolls? She knew Laura would pretend it was an accident, but it wouldn't be.

"They can play with Willie's playthings," Nellie said quickly.

"They can't ride on my velocipede!" Willie shouted.

"Well, they can play with your Noah's ark and your soldiers," Nellie said.

"But they're mine!" Willie yelled.

"Willie, be quiet," Mrs. Oleson said. "This is your sister's party. Go help your father in the store for a while."

"But—" Willie started to protest.

"Go," Mrs. Oleson said, turning him and giving him a shove toward the door.

Nellie brought out the Noah's ark that Willie hardly ever played with. It was a real wooden boat, tall enough to nearly reach Nellie's knees. There were smartly carved little wooden animals to go in it—a pair of zebras, a pair of dogs, elephants, lions, rabbits, horses—every animal you could imagine. All the girls crowded around to marvel at it. Nellie knelt down and marched a pair of tigers up the ramp and onto the boat. Christy squealed and made the rabbits go marching after.

"We'd better add some other animals quick before the tigers eat the rabbits," Christy said, and Laura and Nellie both laughed.

"Maybe the elephants would be good protection," Laura said, kneeling next to her.

"Or the horses," Nellie said, jumping in fast. She grabbed one horse, and Laura took the other.

"What dear little horses," Laura said. "Look at their hooves! And their tails! This red one looks just like Sam, our Christmas horse."

"What's a Christmas horse?" Christy asked.

"We got horses for Christmas this year because Pa wanted them, so we all wished for them," Laura said. "Their names are Sam and David. They're gentle and sweet and beautiful. I love horses, don't you, Nellie?"

"I got a doll for Christmas," Nellie said. "The most beautiful doll in the world. Maybe I'll let you see her later." She jumped to her feet. "My brother has tin soldiers, too. Wait until you see those." She brought out his box of soldiers and dumped them all on the floor. She didn't think the soldiers were as exciting as dolls, but all the girls went "Oooh!" and picked them up and admired their shiny black boots and bright painted uniforms.

Then Nellie brought out Willie's jumping-jack and showed them how it could dance and turn somersaults. Christy started laughing, and her giggles made all the other girls start laughing, too. It was the best feeling Nellie had ever felt. She made the jumping-jack dance and wiggle and flip while all the girls laughed and laughed, and it was all because of her.

If they thought *this* was special, Nellie thought, wait until they saw *her* toys.

She led the girls into the bedroom and got her china doll out of the dresser. She held it out, saying, "You can look at my doll."

"Oh my goodness," Christy said. "All I have is a rag doll. I've never seen a doll like this before."

"Oh!" Laura said. "Oh, what a beautiful doll! Oh, Nellie, what is her name?"

Nellie felt a fiery blush crawl across her cheeks. She had not noticed before that her china doll had the same name as Laura Ingalls.

She had not played with her old doll since she had gotten Guinevere. And Laura Ingalls was so different from Nellie's aunt Laura and her china doll, Laura, that she had never thought about them having the same name. But now she was embarrassed. She did not want Laura Ingalls to think that this doll was named after her. She did not even want her to know that they had the same name. That might make Laura feel special, and this was Nellie's day to feel special. Suddenly she didn't like her china doll quite so much anymore.

"She's nothing but an old doll," Nellie said. She tossed her curls. "I don't care about this old doll. You wait till you see my wax doll." Nellie threw Laura the china doll in a drawer and pulled out Guinevere's box. She put it on the bed and took off the lid slowly, so everyone could lean in and see Guinevere while she still looked like she was sleeping.

Nellie heard a gasp of awe from all the girls except Laura. She lifted Guinevere up and heard another gasp as the doll went "Mamma!" and opened her eyes. She knew this was the most amazing doll any of them had ever seen. She hoped Laura felt silly for being so admiring of a mere china doll.

"Oh, Nellie, I love her," Christy said. "She looks so real!"

"Look how her eyes open and close!" Maud said. "And she talks!"

"Mamma!" said Guinevere.

"She does that when I squeeze her stomach," Nellie said. "Look!" And suddenly she found herself, like Willie, punching the doll in the stomach with her fist.

"Mamma!" cried the doll. Nellie wasn't sure why she did it. She'd never punched Guinevere before. Maybe she just wanted to let all the girls know that she could do anything she wanted with her magnificent toys.

But she did feel a little sorry about it. She saw the look on Laura's face, like Laura was thinking, *If that were my doll, I'd take much better care of her, and I would love her and protect her always.* Nellie thought, *You will* never *have a doll this nice, Laura Ingalls.* At least Laura did not say anything. She only stared at the doll with a wondering expression.

"Her shoes look real, too," said Rosemary. "Do they come off?"

Nellie showed them how the petticoats and drawers and shoes were all real separate parts that you could put on and take off, like their own clothes. Then, as Nellie was smoothing down Guinevere's skirts, she saw Laura reach out a hand toward Guinevere's blue silk dress.

Nellie snatched the doll up against her and held her far away from Laura's dirty, poor, country-girl hands. *Nobody* could touch Guinevere except Nellie, *nobody*. Least of all Nellie's enemy, the girl who had stolen her best friend and turned everyone against her and left Nellie crying in the schoolhouse by herself for an entire recess.

"Don't you touch her!" Nellie yelled. "You keep your hands off my doll, Laura Ingalls!"

She turned quickly and laid Guinevere back in her box. She carefully put the lid back on. She knew the other girls were looking at one another behind her back. Nobody said anything while she put the box back in its drawer.

When she turned around, Laura had gone to sit on a chair and was looking hard at her hands instead of at Nellie.

Nellie was glad. She was happy to see Laura sitting by herself. Now perhaps Nellie could really enjoy her own party.

She led the girls back to the soldiers and the Noah's ark animals. But they seemed quieter than before, and they did not laugh very much at the jumping-jack. At least nobody went over to talk to Laura. *That's because it is* my *party*, Nellie thought. *This is how it should always be.*

After a while Nellie saw her mother give Laura two books to read. One of them was Nellie's own Mother Goose book. But Nellie did not make a fuss. If Laura would stay quietly out of the way, Nellie didn't mind what she did. She began to feel happy again. She showed the other girls the nutcracker, which had been glued back together but still looked a little crooked and dented. She showed them her paper dolls but didn't let the girls play with them in case they tore.

Finally her mother said, "It's time for cake, girls."

Everyone scrambled over to the table, which was covered with a white cloth and set with tiny china plates and tall glasses. In the center of the table was the beautiful sugar-white cake. Mrs. Oleson had added another layer of frosting, and it seemed to sparkle with tiny crystals.

Mrs. Oleson brought Laura over to the table as well, but Laura wouldn't meet Nellie's eyes. She sat quietly in her chair and didn't talk. Nellie thought this was exactly how she liked Laura to be.

A large slice was already cut out of the cake, and Nellie grabbed it as soon as she sat down. "I got the biggest piece!" she announced. Her mother smiled, and Nellie smiled back. This was what it meant to be the hostess of the party. She got everything she wanted.

Mrs. Oleson served the cake to the other girls and poured out lemonade in the tall glasses. Nellie drank her lemonade all the way to the bottom and then ate her cake, which was sweet and crunchy and crumbly in all the right places. Surely it had to be the best cake ever made in Walnut Grove.

The other girls seemed to like it, too. They all ate every last crumb of the slices they were given, even Laura.

After that it was time for everyone to leave. The girls said good-by and thank you in polite company voices. Even Laura Ingalls said, "I had a very good time at the party," to Nellie's mother. But she did not say anything to Nellie.

Mrs. Oleson closed the door. It was quiet now in the parlor. There were dusty footprints on the carpet and books and toys all over the floor. There were plates and glasses to be washed. There was a lot of cleaning to do.

Nellie's mother began tidying briskly. "Come on, Nellie," she said. "Thank goodness that's over with."

"Wasn't it a good party, Mother?" Nellie said.

"It was very nice," Mrs. Oleson said. "I always forget how messy things are afterward. Go put Willie's soldiers back in that box."

"But they're Willie's toys," Nellie said. "Shouldn't he clean them up?"

Mrs. Oleson gave her a stern look. "You made this mess, remember?" she said. "Change out of your nice dress first. We don't want it to get all dusty."

Nellie went slowly back into the bedroom. She wished the party could have kept going. Now she had nothing to look forward to. Her mother would go back to the store accounts. At school on Monday, things would be back to normal.

But maybe everyone would still be talking about her party. And they'd say how wonderful it must be to be Nellie Oleson, and they'd wish they had toys and dolls like hers. And they'd be nice to her again, and she'd play with them at recess and she wouldn't even make them play ring-around-a-rosy, because she knew she'd won in a different way.

Nellie tossed her head and flounced her curls in the looking-glass. She admired her pretty dress one last time before taking it off. She was still the prettiest, richest girl in Walnut Grove, and the only one who had ever thrown a party. Surely everyone would remember it always.

COUNTRY PARTY

Nellie's happiness lasted until recess on Monday. All the girls were talking about her party. They talked about the Noah's ark and the jumping-jack and her marvelous wax doll.

But then Laura Ingalls said, "Mary and I are going to have a party, too, out at our little house by Plum Creek. It will be a week from Saturday." Nellie's mouth dropped open. Laura was stealing her party idea!

"Will you come to my party, Christy?" asked Laura.

"Of course!" Christy said, with much more

excitement than she had shown for Nellie's party.

"What about you, Nellie?" Laura asked. "Will you come to my party?"

Laura's face was open and honest-looking. But surely she was doing this on purpose, Nellie thought. She must have decided to have a party just to show up Nellie. She knew that Nellie's party had made the other girls want to be friends with her. Now she was trying to steal them again with her own party. There was no other explanation.

But Nellie couldn't say no. She didn't want to miss the fun. And she knew it would be worse if she did not go, and then everyone told stories about the party that she would not understand. She would be left out more than ever. That was probably what Laura was hoping for. She wanted Nellie to have no friends at all.

Nellie lifted her nose in the air. "I suppose I will come to your party," she said. "I won't expect it to be as nice as *my* party, of course."

"I am sure it will be very different," Laura said politely. Nellie scowled. What did that mean? Did Laura think her party would be better than Nellie's party? But the Ingalls family was poor. What would they even have to eat at a country party? Did Laura have any toys for them to play with? What would they do?

The other girls had not even had a whole day to talk about Nellie's wonderful party. But now they were already excited about Laura's. It wasn't fair.

"I cannot believe Laura is doing this," Nellie whispered to Christy while Teacher was writing on the blackboard.

"What do you mean?" Christy whispered back.

"Having a party just like mine!" Nellie said. "She is copying me."

"Nellie, don't be silly," Christy said. "Anyone can have a party. I wish *I* could have one, but my mother says there is barely enough room for us Kennedy children in one house as it is. We could never fit in all my friends as well."

Nellie was always surprised by how casually Christy talked about being poor, as if she didn't even know what she was saying about herself.

"But it's not fair," Nellie tried again. "I'm

the one who thought of it first."

"Well, you don't have to go," Christy pointed out. "I'm sure we'll have just as much fun without you there."

Nellie was stung. She turned away from Christy and pretended to be studying her reader very intently. She *was* going to go to Laura's party. She was going to see exactly how Laura lived in her poor country house. She would play with the other girls and eat whatever Mrs. Ingalls gave them. But she wasn't going to have any fun.

Mrs. Oleson was not as offended as Nellie about Laura's party. She even seemed pleased. "I'm glad to see someone in this town has some manners," Nellie's mother said.

"But she stole my idea!" Nellie said.

"How preposterous, Nellie. It is only polite for them to have a party in return. Of course it will be just a country party, but you will be a little lady about it, understand?"

"Fine," Nellie said, crossing her arms and scowling. "Then I want a new dress to wear."

"I think that's a good idea," Mrs. Oleson

said. "Let's look at the new boughten dresses that have come in."

It cheered Nellie up to look through dresses with her mother. They found one that needed only a few adjustments to fit perfectly. Nellie's mother sat down at her sewing machine to bring up the hem.

But Nellie was still disappointed. She had hoped that her mother would agree with her that Laura was a spoilsport. She had hoped it would give her the feeling again of being on the same side as her mother. Instead Mrs. Oleson busied herself with sewing the dress, and Nellie had to play quietly by herself.

All the girls in school talked about Laura's party. They made a plan to walk to Laura's house together, because it was a long way away. Nellie sniffed and turned up her nose whenever they talked about walking so far. She made it plain what *she* thought of living so far from town.

Finally the dreaded Saturday came. Nellie put on her new dress, which was light morning-sky blue with little white daisies on it. She had matching new blue hair ribbons. Once again her shoes were polished to an extra shine.

She met Christy and Maud and the other girls outside the blacksmith shop. Nellie never liked being near the smithy. It was hot and smoky and smelled like things burning that shouldn't be burned. She was always afraid that one day the sparks would fly far enough to set her dress on fire.

Christy led the way out of town to a road that wasn't really a road. It was just wagon wheel tracks in the grass. The tracks led out into the prairie and on and on under the open sky. Nellie could not see any buildings anywhere. She saw nothing but grass and sky up ahead. She felt a little bit afraid. There was so much open space. What if it rained and they all got wet because there was no shelter for miles? What if they lost the road? What if they ended up walking on the wide prairie forever and nobody ever found them?

Then at least we won't have to go to Laura's party, she told herself. She would not show that she was afraid. She squared her shoulders and lifted her chin.

"Of course we must take a country road to a country party," Nellie said. "They don't have real roads or real houses like we do in town."

"Laura has a real house!" Christy said. "You'll see."

They walked and walked for a very long time. Nellie was glad she had her blue sunbonnet to protect her skin. She kept her hands tucked into her pockets so they would not be exposed to the sun either. She carefully walked around anthills and holes in the ground, so no bugs or strange animals could climb on her. She kept her eyes down on the road the whole way, and that was why she did not see Laura's house until the other girls stopped and went, "Ooooooh!"

Nellie looked up. Around her was a sea of waving green wheat. Directly ahead was a bubbling little creek where the sun sparkled off the dancing water. Beyond that was a knoll, and at the top of the hill was a golden house.

Nellie had to stare at the house for a moment before she realized it was not really golden. The walls were made of new sawed lumber, yellow as wheat, and it only looked gold in the sunshine. Light glinted off the glass windows, and a merry puff of smoke came out of the stovepipe chimney.

Laura was racing down the hill toward them, her brown braids flying out behind her. At her heels was a brown-and-white bulldog with a stumpy tail. They both had big smiles on their faces.

Christy waded into the creek first, laughing as her bare feet splashed across the stones. The other girls followed right behind her. Rosemary kicked a splash of water at Maud, and they both shrieked and giggled.

Nellie stood looking at the creek for a moment. No one had told her she had to get wet. She did not want to ruin her shoes and stockings. She would have to take them off, so everyone would have to wait for her.

She searched around until she found a smooth, flat rock to sit on. She did not want to get grass stains on her dress. Then she took off her shoes and stockings and followed the others into the creek.

She didn't understand why they all seemed so happy about the creek. The water was icy cold and tingled against her skin. She wasn't used to walking without shoes, so her bare feet were soft and sensitive. The sharp, hard pebbles at the bottom of the creek stabbed her feet and made her limp. On the other side, the girls were clustered around Laura, exclaiming about the house. Nobody noticed Nellie's troubles getting across the creek.

"Ow!" Nellie cried loudly. "These stones are so hard! The gravel hurts my feet!"

Christy came to help Nellie step out of the water onto the soft grass. Immediately Nellie sat down to put her shoes back on. "I don't go barefooted," she announced. "I have shoes and stockings." *And so should all of you*, she thought. They shouldn't think they were so special just because they could walk across a creek without hurting their feet.

"Is that Jack?" Christy said to Laura, pointing at the dog.

"Yes," Laura said. "He's a very good dog. You can all pet him."

Jack's tongue was long and red and hung down as he panted. His paws were muddy from splashing around at the edge of the creek. His fur was clean and short, but he smelled like a dog, and Nellie had not met very many dogs in her life. She didn't like the size of his teeth or how strong and energetic he was. She didn't know what he might do. She knew that some dogs bit children. Maybe Laura would even tell him to bite Nellie. Nellie was a little afraid of Jack, but she didn't want the other girls to know.

He bounded up to her with his tail wagging like mad, and she was sure he was about to leap up and plant his large muddy paws on her clean new dress. With a squeal, she jumped back. "Go away!" she cried. "Don't you touch my dress!"

"Jack wouldn't touch your dress," Laura said in a proud, scornful way. It was as if she knew that Nellie was afraid of Jack and she thought Nellie was being a baby. Nellie scowled. Just because she didn't want to touch a fierce, dirty animal didn't mean Laura was better than her!

All the girls walked up to the top of the hill, where Mrs. Ingalls stood at the door holding the little blond girl Nellie had seen at the store.

"This is Ma," Laura said. "And this is my baby sister, Carrie."

Carrie reached her hands out toward Nellie's hair ribbons, burbling, "Pretty, pretty." Nellie didn't get too close, but secretly she was pleased that the little girl had noticed her specially.

"Hello, girls," Mrs. Ingalls said. "I am so glad you came to Laura and Mary's party." When she smiled, Nellie believed that she was telling the truth. She did seem happy to see them all. She did not seem flustered or stern or businesslike the way Nellie's mother did.

Mary introduced each of them one by one. When they came to Nellie, Mrs. Ingalls said, "Why, Nellie Oleson. I've visited your father's store. It is nice to meet you—don't you look lovely in that dress?"

Nellie smoothed down the blue cloth and said, "Of course I didn't wear my best dress to just a country party." She wanted Mrs. Ingalls to know she had even prettier dresses at home, like the one she had worn to her own party.

"It's a very pretty dress, Nellie," Mrs. Ingalls

said, smiling. "We're glad you could come."

Nellie liked that. She didn't want to, but she liked the kind way Mrs. Ingalls smiled. She noticed that Laura was frowning, and she wondered if Laura was jealous that her mother clearly liked Nellie so much.

Laura and Mary led the way into the house. White curtains with pink edges fluttered at all the glass windows, which were propped open with sticks so that sunlight and wind poured in. Out here on the prairie, the breeze seemed lighter and less dusty than it did in town. The house was spotlessly clean, and Nellie realized that Laura and Mary must have spent a long time helping their mother clean, just as Nellie had for her own party.

She was surprised at how big the house was. She had still been imagining that the Ingallses lived in a hole in the side of the riverbank. This house was too pretty and clean for her idea of Laura Ingalls. Nellie noticed that the doors had boughten hinges and locks with white china door knobs. Mr. Ingalls had probably bought them at her father's store.

Laura showed them all around the house. To the left when they came in was a bedroom for Mr. and Mrs. Ingalls and Carrie. Straight ahead, a back door led to a lean-to with a black iron cookstove in it like the one Mrs. Oleson used. The girls saw a set of short boards nailed in a row up the wall like a ladder.

Laura went straight to this ladder and climbed up fearlessly. She jumped through the hole up above and called down. "Come up and see our room!"

The girls looked at each other nervously. Christy was the first to climb up. Laura helped her step from the ladder to the attic floor. Then the other girls followed one by one. Nellie waited to be last. She wanted to see how they all got off the ladder upstairs. She didn't want to show that it scared her.

When she got to the top, Laura was at the other end of the room and did not come to help Nellie off the ladder. It took Nellie a minute to gather her courage, but then she stepped off onto the floor, which was made of smooth fitted boards. The attic room was the size of the entire house, wide and open with two glass windows. Up above, the slanted ceiling was made of the bottoms of the roof shingles.

Nellie saw that the room had no dresser, and there was nothing with drawers like the bedroom in her house. The Ingallses probably could not afford a dresser, and there would be no way to get it up the ladder, anyway. They must have built the bed up here in the attic. But where did they keep their clothes and toys? There were two boxes at the foot of the bed. And one corner of the room had a clean white sheet strung across it. Nellie longed to open the boxes and pull aside the sheet, but something about the clean spareness of the room made her too shy to touch anything.

"All this space is just for you and Mary?" Christy marveled.

"Yes," Laura said proudly. "The only sad thing is that Jack cannot climb the ladder to get up here."

"I wish I had a room like this," Maud said.

"I wish I had a *house* like this!" Rosemary agreed.

Nellie had not expected the girls to like Laura's house so much. She had thought it wouldn't begin to compare to hers. And it was true, there was not a lot to see in the Ingalls house. Most of the furniture had been made by hand, and even the decorations, like the starry paper lining the shelves downstairs, were hand-made. There were no boughten carpets or paintings like Nellie had. But standing in this open, airy room made Nellie feel as if her own house was too cluttered.

It made her curious about Laura's toys. Would they be anything like Nellie's? Surely she could not afford beautiful dolls such as Nellie had, or cunning toys like Willie's. Whatever she had, Nellie wanted to see them.

"Where are your dolls?" she asked.

Laura lifted her chin in a way that reminded Nellie of herself. "I don't play with dolls," she said, as if only very little girls played with dolls. "I play in the creek."

"Oooh, I want to play in the creek!" Christy squealed.

"Me too!" clamored the other girls.

Nellie did not particularly want to go to the creek. Why didn't Laura play with dolls? Was she saying that Nellie was a baby for still playing with them? Or was it because Laura's family couldn't afford any dolls?

As the other girls went down the ladder, Nellie stood and looked around the attic room. She wondered what it would be like to live in such a house. What would it be like to have a farmer for a father, instead of a shopkeeper? She thought it would be very sad not to have all the toys and dolls and dresses and candy that she wanted.

But Laura didn't seem sad. She was as proud of her house as Nellie was of her own. It was hard to understand. Mrs. Oleson had always told Nellie how lucky she was to be rich. Did Laura think she was lucky, too, but for different reasons?

It made Nellie's head hurt to think about. She hurried over to the ladder and followed the other girls downstairs and outside.

A Mean Trick

Nellie did not think she would like the creek or the sunshine or the grass around Laura's house. She did not care about seeing Mrs. Ingalls' garden or Mr. Ingalls' wheat-field or the haystacks or the stable. But when Laura showed them a family of tiny chicks living near the haystacks, even Nellie was delighted. And when they all ran down to the pool where the creek burbled under a footbridge and a great willow tree, Nellie found herself running excitedly with the rest of them.

She took off her shoes and stockings and

put them on a tall rock, where they would stay dry. Then she lifted her skirts above her knees like the other girls and waded into the water. Christy kept chasing minnows and giggling as they darted away. Laura touched Christy's shoulder and yelled, "Tag! You're it!" She ran splashing out of the water and across the footbridge with Christy chasing her.

The sun was warm on Nellie's golden hair. She had left her sunbonnet in the house, like the other girls. The water swirled around her knees, cool and clear, and she wiggled her toes in the soft sand below the surface. She'd never stood barefoot in sand before. She wasn't sure if she liked it. But when she lifted her foot, the sand slid off in a whirl of fuzzy water until she could see her clean pale skin again. It was strange to have something as clean as water and something as dirty as sand together in one place.

Suddenly a hand tapped her back.

"Tag!" Christy cried from behind her. She was already backing away. "Nellie's it!"

Nellie chased Christy up onto the bank and through the warm grass. Some of the girls ran over the footbridge, but Maud splashed into the water and Nellie was able to catch her there.

In the shallowest water around the edge, the bigger girls were playing with Carrie. On the other side of the footbridge from the pool, the creek wandered into a thicket of plum trees that leaned over the water like the rafters of a church. The water there was deeper and darker, and the floor of the creek was mud instead of sand and pebbles.

After they had played tag for a while, Laura picked up her skirts and waded into the pool again. The others followed her over to a big flat rock that was under the water. Laura turned and bumped into Nellie, making Nellie move back toward the rock to keep her balance. Suddenly Laura made an almighty splash with her feet and screamed, "Oo, Nellie! Nellie, look out!"

Nellie jumped, frightened, and then shrieked with terror as she saw a creature running at her under the water. It was sharp-looking, like it was made of a hard shell, with two large snapping claws and a scaly tail and short bristling legs. Nellie had never seen anything so scary in her whole life, and it was running right at her!

The creature snapped its claws at her toes like it was going to clip them off. Nellie screamed again and tried to run, but the water caught at her skirts and dragged at her petticoats so she couldn't run very fast.

"Run! Run!" Laura yelled. Nellie didn't see where the other girls ran, but with Laura behind her, she ran all the way to the dark water under the plum thicket, as far as she could get from the scaly snapping monster.

When she turned around, Laura was still standing out in the sun, looking at the rock where it had come from.

"Wait, Nellie," she said. "You stay there." She stood between Nellie and the rock. She looked like she was protecting Nellie from the animal.

"Oh, what was it? What was it?" Nellie asked. Her heart was beating so fast, she thought it might try to gallop out of her chest. Her whole body was shaking. She had dropped her skirts into the muddy water, but she was too afraid to care. "Is he coming?"

"It's an old crab," Laura said. "He cuts big sticks in two with his claws. He could cut our toes right off."

Nellie couldn't believe Laura had let them play in the water with such a dangerous animal close by. She pictured the crab again in her mind and shivered. How fast could he move? How far would he go? Was he coming after her?

"Oh, where is he?" she said. "Is he coming?"

"You stay there and I'll look," said Laura. She walked slowly through the water, peering down at the swirling sand. She looked very intent. Nellie was surprised at how brave Laura was. She did not seem worried about the crab biting off her own toes. She was only trying to help Nellie. Maybe Laura Ingalls was not so bad after all.

But that did not make her house or her creek a safe place to be. Now Nellie remembered why she hated the prairie and the whole outdoors.

Nellie shivered again. Under the plum thicket the water was colder, and she couldn't see the bottom of the creek through the thick mud that sucked at her feet and swirled about her legs. Mosquitoes swarmed around her, and water bugs skated past. She tried to slap away the mosquitoes, but she knew they were sneaking past to bite her. She felt like insects were crawling all over her, and she just wanted to go home and be in her nice, clean, safe, dry house again.

Finally Laura came wading back. "You can come out now," she said.

Nellie splashed back into the sunnier, warmer water. "I hate this horrid old creek," she said. "This is the worst party I've ever been to. I wish we had just stayed inside with dolls." She looked down and saw the muddy edges of her new dress and petticoats. Her mother was going to be furious with her. She would know that Nellie had been playing outside, and she would be angry about having to wash her new dress. She would tell Nellie that a proper lady never got her dress muddy or went wading in horrid creeks.

Tears prickled at the back of Nellie's eyes. "I don't want to play anymore," she said. She reached down and rubbed her skirt in the water, trying to wash off the mud. Below the clear surface of the water, she saw, she had clumps of mud stuck to her feet. They hadn't washed off like the sand in the sunnier part of the pool. She lifted one foot and tried to brush off the mud.

The blobs were brown and soft and felt like mud, but they would not come off. They were stuck to her skin! She put two fingers around one and tried to pick it off, but it just seemed to stick tighter with a squashy wobble. It was alive! She had horrible mudlike *things* stuck all over her feet!

Nellie screamed and screamed. She'd never seen anything like this. She was even more scared than when the crab had attacked her.

She ran screaming up onto the creek bank and kicked her feet, trying to shake them off. There were so many! She could see that some were as high as her knees.

"Oh, help!" Nellie shrieked. "It's horrible! Somebody help me!" Every little bit of her was terrified. What if they never came off?

But when she looked up, Laura was rolling on the grass and laughing. "Oh, look, look!" Laura called. She pointed at Nellie, laughing so hard she couldn't even stand up. "See Nellie dance!"

Nellie stopped jumping. She started crying. It had all been a trick. Laura had tricked her. She had scared Nellie with the crab and gotten Nellie covered with sickening brown worms. Nellie thought she had never heard of a meaner trick. Surely this was the worst thing anyone could do to somebody, ever.

The other girls came running over. Mary looked appalled. She pressed both hands to her face and made a round "O" with her mouth.

"Laura!" Mary said. "Take those blood-suckers off Nellie right now!"

Nellie cried harder. Bloodsuckers? Were they sucking her blood right now? What if they sucked it all out? Was she going to die?

Laura was still laughing. She kept falling over in the grass and laughing harder. Nellie was sure now that Laura was the meanest girl she had ever met. Nellie thought she was good at mean tricks herself, but she would never have thought of something this awful.

"Laura!" Mary said. "You get up and pull those things off, or I'll tell Ma."

Laura finally got up. She pinched one of the blobs between her fingers. She pulled it away from Nellie's skin so it stretched out—longer and longer and longer. It wouldn't come off! And then, suddenly, it came free with a *squick*. A thin trickle of blood ran down Nellie's leg where it had been.

Nellie saw the blood and screamed again. Maud and Becky screamed, too.

"Stop screaming, Nellie," Laura said, but not in a nice voice. "They're just leeches. They won't kill you."

Nellie looked up and saw Christy watching with wide eyes. Did she see what Laura was really like now? As Laura pulled another bloodsucker off, the other girls all screamed again. Nellie was sure that Laura was going as slowly as possible to torture Nellie. She dragged each leech out as long as it could get before it popped off. Nellie's legs were covered in tiny rivers of blood.

"I don't like your party!" Nellie sobbed. "I want to go home!"

"Don't worry, Nellie," Mary said. "Ma will take care of you."

Mrs. Ingalls was hurrying down the hill from the house with a worried expression. She had heard all the girls screaming. Laura and Mary told her what had happened to Nellie. They didn't say that it was Laura's fault. Mrs. Ingalls knelt down, and Nellie looked into her kind face.

"I want to go home!" Nellie wailed. "I hate the country! I want to go home!"

"Now, now, stop crying," Mrs. Ingalls said briskly. "A few leeches are nothing to cry about, Nellie." Nellie swallowed her sobs, feeling hurt. She had wanted Mrs. Ingalls to feel sorry for her, but instead Laura's mother acted like Nellie was upset over nothing.

Mrs. Ingalls used clear water from the creek to wash the blood off Nellie's legs. While Nellie put her stockings and shoes back on, Mrs. Ingalls said, "It's time for everyone to come back up to the house."

The girls ran chattering back up the hill. Nellie followed them slowly. No one stayed behind to walk with her. No one made sure she was all right. She wanted to turn around and march right back to town. But she was afraid she would get lost on the prairie. She needed to wait for the other girls to walk with her.

She was too mad to speak. Why would Laura be so mean to her? How could Nellie get her revenge? She felt too upset to plan any clever tricks. She just wanted to go home.

Inside the airy house a white cloth was spread over the table, and a blue pitcher of flowers was set in the center. The girls sat on benches along either side. Mrs. Ingalls gave them each a tin cup full of milk. She served them from a platter piled high with puffy, honey-colored cakes.

Nellie turned her tin cup in her hands. It was very common, much uglier than the pretty glasses she used at home. She took a bite of the cake and nearly spat it out. It didn't taste like honey at all! It wasn't even sweet! It was just crispy and full of air, like eating nothing. What a strange cake.

She looked at the other girls, but they were all eating happily. Christy said, "I've never eaten anything this good before in my life." That made Nellie even madder. The cake at her party had been much better! It was sweet and had sugar-white frosting on it that she had helped make herself! How could Christy like this nothing cake better than Nellie's special sweet one?

"What are they called?" Maud asked.

"Vanity cakes," Mrs. Ingalls said. "Because they are all puffed up, like vanity, with nothing solid inside."

Nellie looked up and saw Mrs. Ingalls watching her. Was she talking about Nellie? Maybe she was calling Nellie vain. Nellie didn't think that was fair. Mrs. Ingalls didn't even know her.

Nellie tried very hard not to cry for the rest of the party. She ate her cake and drank her milk and didn't talk to the other girls. Finally they had eaten everything, and everyone got up to leave.

"Thank you very much, Mrs. Ingalls," Christy said. "We had a very nice time."

"I'm so glad you all came," Laura's mother said.

The other girls all thanked her, too. Nellie wouldn't look at Laura or her mother. She wouldn't say thank you. She had nothing to thank them for. It had been the worst party and the worst day of her life.

As she walked down the hill, Nellie turned back and saw Laura and Mary and Mrs. Ingalls and Carrie standing at the door. Carrie was waving happily. Laura had a gleeful smile on her face.

I will never forgive you for this, Laura Ingalls, Nellie thought. She remembered the Dawsons leaving the year before. She wished very hard that something terrible would happen so the Ingallses would have to leave, too. Then she could have her town and her school and her friends back again. *You are my enemy forever, Laura. I hope something really, really dreadful happens to you.*

The Grasshoppers Come

The days stretched on, getting longer and hotter all the time. Laura and Mary started coming to church and Sunday school, which meant Nellie had to see Laura six days a week.

The heat was unbearable. Nellie's dresses stuck to her skin as soon as she put them on. Her hair drooped and clung to her neck in wet curls. Her stockings and petticoats felt like they were dragging her down. She longed to take off her shoes and let her bare feet get some air, but after the leech incident she had promised her mother not to take them off in front of people again.

It was hard to concentrate on lessons. All the children in the schoolhouse were dripping in the heat. The bigger boys sweated and smelled awful. Everything itched, and flies flew through the open windows to crawl all over the desks. The benches and the walls were sticky. When they first came inside in the morning, before the windows were open, it felt to Nellie like she was standing in her mother's cookstove.

Teacher called each class to the front every hour to drink a dipper full of water. During recess the girls stayed in the shade of the schoolhouse. It was too hot to run around and play. Nellie was glad. She did not want to play any more of Laura's games.

Nellie wished she could think of a good revenge against Laura. But she was too hot to think straight. The heat made her tired. She couldn't sleep at night because of the heat pressing down against the walls of the house.

She thought about New York again. She thought about sweet ice cream and the wind coming off the harbor. She thought about the smell of the sea and the tall ships with their billowing white sails. She thought of elegant ladies with parasols and fans, traveling the streets by carriage and staying out of the sun. She knew she should be one of them.

But with every day, she felt more and more trapped in Walnut Grove. She felt as if she would always be here. She would always have to see Laura's face and hear her whispering with Christy during recess. She would be stuck here with the heat and the insects and the choking dust forever.

Nellie was feeling very sorry for herself.

One Saturday Nellie was finishing dinner with her mother and Willie. Her father was out front running the store. After she had eaten, Mrs. Oleson would run the store while her husband ate his dinner.

Sunshine was pouring through the glass windows and dancing in yellow streaks across the rug. Nellie propped her head on her hand and watched the light. She felt dazed and sleepy. Her eyelids drooped. The sunlight got dimmer.

Nellie opened her eyes wide. The light was

still getting dimmer. Clouds must be coming up fast. Perhaps a storm would break the heat and beat down the dust.

She got up and went to the window. The sky in the distance was dark and glittering. The sun was covered by a strange cloud. It did not look like storm clouds.

Mr. Oleson burst into the parlor.

"Grasshoppers!" he cried. "Grasshoppers are coming!"

"Grasshoppers?" Nellie said. She remembered the long, ugly insect she had picked out of Teacher's desk. It was a vile creature, but she didn't know why her father sounded so alarmed.

Nellie's mother was standing up, twisting a white linen napkin in her hands.

"What's the matter, William?" she asked. "What do you mean?"

"Come look outside," he said, and they all followed him into the store. A group of men had gathered by the front door, looking out.

Nellie could hear a strange noise now. It sounded like someone rubbing violin bows together. It sounded like buzzing and whirring and a high-pitched whine at the same time. She clapped her hands to her ears, trying to keep out the peculiar piercing sound.

Mr. Oleson and Willie followed the other men onto the street. Nellie and her mother stood in the doorway. The air was hot and still, and the flickering cloud was getting closer and closer.

Plop! Plop! Plop! Suddenly grasshoppers were falling from the sky. They were enormous and squirming. Their eyes bulged out of their heads like the eyes on the crab that had chased Nellie. They rained down faster and faster, covering the street and sliding over roofs and ledges. Willie yelled with surprise and began stamping on them. Grasshoppers squished and crunched beneath his shoes. But more and more kept coming.

"Back into the store!" Mr. Oleson barked, pushing Willie, Nellie, and her mother inside. "Make sure all the windows are closed! Shut the door and bar it! No one comes in until this storm of insects has passed. I will not have grasshoppers in my store!"

Mrs. Oleson ran back to the parlor to close all the windows and the back door. Mr. Oleson slammed the front door of the general store. Two of the men came back and hammered on it, demanding the goods they had come to buy. But Mr. Oleson called through the door, "Come back later! When the grasshoppers are gone!"

Nellie watched as her father tacked up a large sheet of cloth to cover the door. He hammered nails around the edges so it was stretched tight. He stuffed the bottom edge into the crack between the door and the floor. If any grasshoppers tried to get through the cracks of the door, they would run into the sheet.

Then he went around the store examining each board and anything that looked like a hole in the wall. He hammered loose boards over every crack.

"We can't take any chances, Nellie," Mr. Oleson said. "This store is everything. The goods in here are our livelihood. We must not let anything happen to them."

Nellie still wasn't sure how the grasshoppers

could hurt her father's store. But as she watched through the glass window, she saw more and more grasshoppers swarming down. A crunching, chewing sound joined the whirring noise. She could see the Gilberts' vegetable garden across the street. As grasshoppers covered the neat rows of plants, all the green disappeared. The grasshoppers ate everything in sight. They chomped their way through the vegetables so fast that Nellie barely saw it happen. One moment there were beans twisting around sticks stuck in the ground, and the next moment they were gone.

Nellie and Willie stayed at the window watching for the rest of the day. Willie thought it was tremendously exciting. He whooped and hollered at every new thing the grasshoppers did. He kept asking their father if they could go out and stomp the grasshoppers. But Mr. Oleson would not let them leave. He would not let them open the doors or windows. He was very stern, and Nellie knew that for once he meant what he said. He was protecting his store and his supplies. That was one thing Mr.

Oleson cared about very much.

It was even hotter with all the windows closed. But at least Nellie did not have to do any chores. Mrs. Oleson did not feel like cooking. She brought her chair to the window and sat watching with them. They ate dried fruit and crackers and sardines from tins at suppertime.

Everything felt strange and unreal. Nellie knew she should be worried, but mostly she felt excited. This was something new, something different. She felt like lightning was crackling inside her. As long as she was safe indoors, it was interesting to watch the chaos made by the grasshoppers. Outside, men ran up and down the streets, covering their heads with shawls or hats and sometimes wading through piles of grasshoppers up to their knees. Every bit of green that Nellie could see was eaten away.

And constantly they could hear the sound of grasshoppers pattering against the roof and chewing and chewing.

Toward the end of the day Willie suddenly jumped off his stool.

"Pa!" he shouted. "Pa, look!"

Grasshoppers were crawling in under the door. They had chewed right through the sheet. They were eating holes in the cloth and marching through the cracks into the store. They would not eat everything, like the salt pork and the candy, but they would eat anything they could. They would eat anything they came across, even cloth.

Nellie jumped up with a shriek. She climbed on her chair and stood there out of the way of the insects. Mr. Oleson grabbed a shovel and began smashing all the grasshoppers on the floor. Willie ran around stomping on the ones that scuttled away, while Mrs. Oleson flattened the ones on the wall with a frying pan.

Then Mr. Oleson ran to get another sheet and nailed it down over the one the grasshoppers had eaten. He took pieces of wood and shoved them into the cracks as well. He blocked off every crack as well as he could.

When Nellie went to bed, her father was still in the store, holding up a lantern and patrolling around the walls to make sure no more grasshoppers tried to come in. She was not sure if he slept at all that night.

The next day was Sunday. But Mr. Oleson would not let them leave the house to go to church. He did not want the door to be open long enough for grasshoppers to come in. He did not want them to bring grasshoppers in on their clothes and in their hair. This sounded like good sense to Nellie. She did not want grasshoppers in her clothes and hair, either. She did not really like Sunday school anyway. She wondered if anyone would go on a day like this.

But being stuck inside the house was not much fun either. Without any customers, Mr. and Mrs. Oleson were snappish and tense. They kept staring out the window. They yelled at Willie for making too much noise. Mrs. Oleson made Nellie sweep the floors and dust inside the store, since she had not done the dusting on Saturday. Nellie did not see the point of this. No one was coming in, so who cared if it was clean?

The faces that passed the window looked worried and pale. Not many people were out on the street. The town was overrun with grasshoppers. It looked like grasshoppers lived in Walnut Grove instead of people.

After a few days Mr. Oleson opened his store again. He knew people needed food, and they needed to get it from the general store now that all the farms and gardens had been ruined. He also knew that they would pay more for things they needed so badly, so he raised his prices. Not by a lot—a nickel here, a penny there. Most people didn't notice. But some folks complained. A few even went to Mr. Beadle's store instead.

"They will come back," Mr. Oleson said. "They need my supplies. They have nothing else to eat. This could be lucky for us, Margaret," he said to Nellie's mother.

He was very strict about people coming in and out. He made them stand outside the door and shake the grasshoppers off their clothes before coming in. He had Willie follow the customers around and stamp on any grasshoppers that fell off them. He kept the door closed and made all the customers shut it fast behind them.

Nellie thought her father was very smart. All the men who came to the store looked tired and worn out. They looked like they had been chasing grasshoppers for days. They looked like ruined men.

Mr. Kennedy came into the store. Nellie knew he depended on his farm to support his wife and five children. He had dark circles under his eyes, and his clothes were stained with brown spots from the grasshoppers. He bought a very small sack of cornmeal, laying out his coins on the counter with a trembling hand.

Some of the men gathered around the stove to talk, although it was too hot for the stove to be lit. They smoked their pipes and stamped their feet and talked in low, worried voices. Nellie stayed away from them. She did not like the smell of the tobacco smoke, and she knew it was not proper for ladies to be seen in such company.

But sometimes while she was dusting the shelves, she could hear what they said. She heard that the grasshoppers had devastated the whole prairie. There were millions of them, for miles and miles around. No one had ever seen such a plague of grasshoppers. Someone said the plague stretched as far west as Oregon and as far south as Kansas and Missouri. Someone else said they were even eating wooden fences and the wool off living sheep. Nellie wasn't sure whether to believe stories like that.

Many of the farmers had tried different ways of killing the grasshoppers, even setting fire to them. But there were too many grasshoppers to wipe them out.

There was still no rain to break the unending heat. Everything was brown and dead and covered in moving brown grasshoppers. Nellie was glad that her father did not make her go outside. She did not have to go to school all that week. Her mother did not want the grasshoppers ruining Nellie's dresses and shoes.

On Wednesday night her father sat down to supper with them. He had a sharp crease between his eyebrows, but he was also smiling. As Mrs. Oleson served the salt pork and corn dodgers, Mr. Oleson lifted his fork and pointed it at Willie and Nellie.

"I hope you children are learning something from all this," he said.

"I am!" said Willie. "I wish I were a grasshopper! They can eat *anything*. I never knew there were so many grasshoppers in the whole world."

"That is not what I mean," Mr. Oleson said, wagging his fork. "I hope you both realize how lucky you are to have a storekeeper for a father. If I were a farmer, like most of these men, we would be ruined right now. The grasshoppers have destroyed everything those farmers worked for. But we have our money in goods and produce, which everyone will always need. We will never be devastated by nature and catastrophes like this."

"You will see a lot of other families suffering because of this plague," said Mrs. Oleson. "Just remember that thanks to your father, we will be all right. This store will last longer than all of those farms out there."

Nellie caught her breath. She had not thought of Laura Ingalls in days. She hadn't once thought about what the grasshoppers might be doing to the Ingalls farm. She had been so caught up in what was happening out the window that she had not sent her thoughts farther out on the prairie.

If the grasshoppers had truly eaten everything, they must have destroyed Laura's father's entire wheat crop. They probably had eaten up all the grass the girls had played in, and the willow tree over the creek, and the plum thicket that cast the shade where Nellie had been attacked by the leeches. There must be nothing left of the Ingallses' carefully tended garden, which Laura had been so proud to show them.

Nellie felt a strange flapping in her chest. She had hoped that something terrible would happen to make the Ingalls family go back east. But she did not feel as happy as she expected to. This plague was much worse than anything she had imagined.

In wishing for something dreadful to happen to Laura's family—had Nellie brought the grasshoppers down on everyone in Walnut Grove?

The Empty Town

Nellie did not see Laura again until Sunday. She came to Sunday school with her father and Mary. They walked into town and left their horses at home instead of driving in on their wagon. Nellie saw that they were all wearing shoes, and she thought how awful it must be to walk over grasshoppers with bare feet. They looked hot and dusty and tired. Mr. Ingalls had the same look as the other farmers, as if his tiredness had permanently settled inside him.

Mrs. Oleson had decided they could go to church, since it was not far to walk. But even in that short time, Nellie felt grasshoppers crawling through her hair and clawing up her petticoats. It was a horrible, creepy feeling. She shook them free on the steps outside the church. When she looked up, she saw Laura and Mary nearby doing the same thing. They had many more grasshoppers on them than Nellie did, because they had walked so much farther. They also had brown stains on their Sunday dresses where the grasshoppers had spit tobacco-juice on them.

Laura was brushing off her skirts. She did not seem to notice Nellie. She looked sad.

Nellie felt the flapping feeling inside again. She did not know why Laura's sadness did not make her happier.

After Sunday school Nellie went up to Christy Kennedy. Christy was also very pale, and her dark eyes kept filling with tears.

"Christy, what is it?" Nellie asked.

"We have to leave," Christy said. "We are going back east. We have lost everything." She started crying again.

Laura went past Nellie and put her arms

around Christy. The two of them hugged and cried and said good-by.

"You are my best friend, Christy," Laura said. "I will miss you."

"You're my best friend, too," Christy said. "Don't forget me."

"Maybe one day you will come back," said Laura.

"Maybe," Christy said, tugging on one of her stiff red braids.

Nellie remembered telling Christy about how she wanted to go back east. She remembered Christy saying that she wanted to go on west, all the way to the other side of the country. It didn't seem fair that they were both getting the opposite of what they wanted. For a moment Nellie wished they could trade places, but she knew she would not really like that, for then she would have to be poor.

"I will miss you, too, Christy," she said awkwardly.

Christy threw her arms around Nellie and hugged her. Nellie was surprised. She patted Christy's back.

"I think there is hope for you, Nellie Oleson," Christy said. "I really do."

Then she turned around and left the church with her sister Cassie and Laura.

Nellie wondered what Christy meant by her remark. Hope for Nellie? It was an odd thing to say. Surely it was poor farmers like Laura and Christy who needed hope.

She went slowly out of the church and down the steps. She saw the Kennedys walking away together through the dry brown dirt where grass had waved eight days before. She watched Christy's bright red hair in the shining light and knew that she would probably never see Christy again.

Nellie wondered if she was being punished. She had brought the grasshoppers with her terrible wishes. But instead of getting rid of Laura, she was losing Christy.

A huge sadness pressed down on Nellie. Now everything was even worse than before. Even the heat seemed worse with nothing green in sight for miles.

At school the next day many students were

missing. Laura and Mary did not make the long walk into town. Nellie guessed that they did not want to walk over the grasshoppers again. They did not come the next day, either, or the day after that. Soon Nellie realized that they were not coming back to school. She tried to be happy about that, too, but with nobody else to play with, it hardly mattered anymore whether Laura was there or not.

Fewer and fewer people came into the store. Half the town had left to go back east. The plague had wiped out all the crops and all the hay for the livestock. All the animals that could go on their own had left, like the rabbits. Farmers had to drive their cattle far, far away to find grass, or else they would starve.

Sometimes Nellie came in from school to find her father standing alone at the counter. He would wipe a dust rag from one end to the other and back again. He stared off into space. Wrinkles lined his forehead.

Mrs. Oleson looked worried, too. She spent all day going through their account books. She hardly spoke to Nellie and Willie. But Nellie didn't know what they were worrying about. Her parents had said themselves that the Olesons would be fine. They had their store. They were still rich. They were much better off than everyone else in town.

There was a lot of talk in the store about getting help from the government. The state of Minnesota wanted to help the farmers who had lost everything to the grasshoppers. Willie heard a man say that the government was paying people to kill grasshoppers. They would pay anyone fifty cents for every bushel of grasshoppers they killed.

This got Willie very excited. He spent days running around outside, chasing grasshoppers. He killed hundreds and hundreds of them and poured the dead, rustling bodies into sacks. Nellie could not believe how many grasshoppers he killed. And yet for every one he killed, there seemed to be another ten thousand out there waiting.

Willie was very proud of his sacks of grasshoppers. He piled them behind the Olesons' lean-to. He collected nearly four whole sacks full of grasshoppers. That was two dollars' worth!

But he didn't know what to do with the sacks. There were no government people in Walnut Grove. Nobody here would pay him for the dead grasshoppers. He tried to talk their father into taking him east so he could trade in his bushels of grasshoppers, but Mr. Oleson said no. He didn't want to leave the store for so long. He did not believe that the government would pay Willie.

Willie stopped killing grasshoppers and spent a few days sulking. Then he and Mr. Oleson dragged the sacks to a clear patch of dirt and set them on fire. Nellie watched from a distance. The grasshoppers made a crackling sound as they went up in flames. They smelled horrible, like leaves rotting.

One day Mr. Ingalls came into the store. He stood with the other men talking around the stove. He told them about finding grasshopper eggs in his field. The grasshoppers had buried their eggs all through the soil for miles and miles. When they hatched, another plague of

grasshoppers would rise up and ruin everything all over again.

Hearing this, Nellie nearly started crying
right there in the store. How would they ever
get rid of all the grasshoppers? If they kept
laying eggs year after year, wouldn't there
always be millions of them? Had her terrible
wish ruined the whole prairie forever?

Mr. Ingalls asked the other men if they
knew of any work. They told him that many
men were going east to help harvest crops out
where the grasshoppers had not reached. The
government was saying it was all right for men
to leave their land, even though they normally
had to live on it to claim it. But now, when
they could not grow any crops of their own,
they were allowed to go elsewhere for work.

Later Nellie heard her father tell her mother
that Mr. Ingalls had decided to go. He would
leave his family here and go east to earn money.
He would be gone for the rest of the summer.
Nellie was glad again that her father was a
storekeeper and did not have to leave them
alone for so long.

Now the Ingallses did not come to Sunday school, either. Days and days passed without any sign of Laura. In a way, Nellie had gotten her wish. The town was all hers now. But it did not matter. Hardly any students came to school. Becky had gone back east. Maud's mother kept her at home to help with her sick younger brothers. During recess, Nellie stayed inside and drew pictures on her slate.

Sometimes Teacher came and sat on the bench beside her. She didn't bother Nellie, only opened a book and read quietly. Nellie liked having her there, so close by. It made her feel a little less alone.

Some weeks after the grasshoppers came, Nellie and Willie went into the store and found their father measuring out coffee beans. He was by himself, so it was not for a customer. He was just checking how much coffee there was.

Willie went up to one of the barrels of candy and reached inside.

Suddenly Mr. Oleson shouted, "NO!"

Willie jumped back. His eyes were round with fright.

"Don't touch that," Mr. Oleson said, banging the lid down on the barrel. "No more candy."

Nellie and Willie were shocked.

"No more candy?" Willie whined. "Why?"

"That is for the customers," their father said gruffly.

"But we always—" Nellie started.

"I know what you always!" Mr. Oleson yelled. "I see how you stuff your faces with the food I pay for!"

Nellie turned and ran back into the parlor. Mrs. Oleson was there, and Nellie could see that she had heard. Her face was white as the curtains.

"Father is being mean!" Nellie cried. "He said before that we could have the candy! He said we could have anything we wanted! I don't understand! It's not fair!"

She kicked the table leg and burst into tears. She threw herself down on the carpet and cried, but her mother did not lift her up.

"It is a hard time," Mrs. Oleson said distantly. "We have to be more careful than usual. We may not have the money to buy more supplies for the store."

"But you said we would be all right," Nellie sniffled. "We own a whole store! We have everything people need."

Mrs. Oleson sat down heavily in one of the chairs. She did not look at Nellie. She picked at a loose thread on her apron. "A lot of people have left town, Nellie," her mother said. "You might have noticed that we don't have as many customers as we used to."

"So?" Nellie said.

"Without customers, we cannot afford to stock the store. So many people are gone, there's hardly anyone left to buy our supplies. We borrowed a lot of money to come out here, and now it will be much harder to pay it back."

Nellie didn't understand. "But we're rich," she said. "We're the richest family in town. Everyone knows that."

Mrs. Oleson exhaled sharply and stood up. "You are too little to understand," she said. "Just be good and do as you're told. Do not take anything from the store without asking us first. We will all have to chip in to make it through these difficult times."

She went back into the kitchen and left Nellie crying on the parlor floor. Willie came through the door, looking subdued. He went straight back to the bedroom and did not come out again until supper. Mr. Oleson did not say anything about shouting at them. He did not say he was sorry. He ate his supper in silence, an angry frown on his face. Nobody said anything the whole meal.

Later that night Nellie lay on her bed surrounded by the hot darkness. She had thought that Laura Ingalls coming to town was the worst thing that could ever happen to her. She had thought that being Christy's best friend was the only thing she could lose. She had thought that the crab and the leeches were as bad as it could get.

Now she knew that things could get much, much worse. Millions of grasshoppers were worse than a few leeches any day. Christy was gone forever. And she could not even rely on being the richest girl in town anymore.

She cried herself to sleep.

Hurried and Sparkling Waters

Weeks went by, and finally a day came when Nellie and Willie were the only students in school. Teacher set her slate down on her desk and smiled at them.

"I think this will be our last week of school," she said. "It's almost time to close for the winter, anyway."

Nellie knew this was true. The rain had finally come and washed away some of the heat. Tiny green tips were poking out all across the prairie. Leaves were growing back on the trees. And the mornings were starting to get colder.

Teacher went over all of Nellie's work in the reader. At the end of the day, she smiled at Nellie. "You have done very well this year," she said. "I am very impressed with you."

Nellie had had lots of time to study. She had not spent as much time playing with the other girls this year. Everything had been so quiet at home. She had not realized that she had learned so much.

After school Nellie went to the store to tell her father what Teacher had said. She found the front door locked. She was surprised but not worried. Her father was probably counting the money in the cash box. She circled around the house and went in through the back entrance and the kitchen. She walked through the door to the store and stopped.

Her father was standing in front of a barrel of coffee beans. He did not have the cash box out. Instead he was holding a small sack and staring into the barrel. He looked as if he had been standing and staring for a long time.

When the door banged behind Nellie, Mr. Oleson jumped. He held the sack to his chest and looked at her for a moment as if he did not know who she was.

"Oh," he said, relaxing slightly. "It's you, Nellie."

"What are you doing?" she asked.

"Nothing," he said. "Go back to the parlor."

"What's in the sack?" she asked.

"Nellie, I told you to go away," he said.

She took a step back and then stopped. There was something about the way her father was standing. He looked like Willie did when he'd done something bad and was about to be caught.

Mr. Oleson dropped his eyes. He put one hand in the sack and pulled out a handful of something. Nellie came over and looked at what he was holding.

At first she thought it was coffee beans. She thought, *Oh, he's just filling a sack with coffee beans.* Then she looked closer. She picked up one of the beans in his hand and rolled it between her fingers.

It was not a coffee bean. It was a dry navy bean, dyed brown to look like coffee.

Nellie looked up at her father. She was confused.

"Sometimes," Mr. Oleson said, "we have to do things that we aren't proud of, Nellie."

He turned and poured the sack of dyed navy beans into the barrel of coffee beans.

"But . . ." Nellie said. "But that's not coffee. Father, won't people be mad that you're giving them beans in their coffee?"

"They won't notice," her father said. "This way it looks like we have more coffee to sell. The price of coffee is higher than the price of beans, which means we can make more money, which we need to pay our debts. A lot of store-keepers do this."

"They do?" Nellie said.

"Yes," said Mr. Oleson. "Some of them even put sawdust in the cornmeal or plaster in the flour to stretch it further. I haven't had to do that yet. But these are desperate times, Nellie. We must do what we can."

Nellie didn't understand. It seemed wrong. Surely this was not something he wanted to do. And what if he got caught? Wouldn't he be in a lot of trouble? It would not be good for his reputation as an honest shopkeeper—Nellie knew that.

"Don't worry, Nellie," Mr. Oleson said. "It is only a few hundred beans. But it will be worth it if we can sell a lot more coffee. Now go back inside and help your mother with supper."

He took a dipper and began stirring the dyed beans into the barrel so they mixed with the coffee beans. He did not look at Nellie again.

Nellie went back into the parlor. She did not know what to do. She wondered if her mother knew what he was doing. She took Guinevere out of her box and sat holding her, but Guinevere couldn't help her with this problem.

The next day in school Teacher sat on the bench next to Nellie and checked her sums in the math book. Nellie watched her and wished she could be grown up. She thought it must be easier than being eight years old.

At recess time Willie ran outdoors to chase prairie chickens around the schoolhouse. Teacher set down her slate pencil and looked at Nellie.

"I get the feeling you have something on

your mind, Nellie," she said. "Do you want to talk about it?"

Nellie shook her head. Teacher was the last person she could talk to about her father. Teacher would surely tell her brother, Mr. Beadle, who would tell everyone in town so that they would come to his store instead.

"Are you sure?" Teacher said. "Sometimes telling what we are worried about can help."

It felt like a giant bubble was swelling up inside Nellie. Teacher was kind, and Teacher was the only friend Nellie still had in Walnut Grove.

"I did it," she blurted out. "It was me. I'm the one who made Willie put the insects in your desk last year." She held her breath. She didn't dare look at Teacher.

"I know," Teacher said quietly.

Nellie's head jerked up. "You do?"

"I guessed," Teacher said. "I hoped that you would come forward and confess. I'll admit I stopped hoping after a while."

"But if you knew," Nellie said, "why didn't you punish me?"

"I didn't think it would do any good,"

Teacher said. "You would only be angrier than before, and I wanted you to decide for yourself what was the right thing to do."

"Oh," Nellie said.

"I'm very glad you did," said Teacher. "That was brave of you. I have great hope for you, Nellie."

It was the same thing Christy had said. Now Nellie understood it a little better. They meant that perhaps one day Nellie would learn to be good and kind and to care about other people.

"I did something else," Nellie said. It was the hardest thing she had ever had to say, even harder than confessing about the bugs. But she wanted to be as brave as Teacher said she was. "I—I made the grasshoppers come," Nellie whispered. Tears rolled down her cheeks.

"Oh, no, Nellie," Teacher said.

"I did," Nellie said. "I wished for something terrible to happen to Laura Ingalls' family. I wanted them to leave Walnut Grove. It's my fault the grasshoppers came and destroyed everything and Christy had to go instead." She cried harder.

"Nellie," Teacher said, and her voice was very firm, "you did not bring the grasshoppers. You are right that it was wrong to wish for something terrible to happen to someone else. But terrible things like this happen all the time. You cannot blame yourself. Everyone has dark thoughts now and then, but the grasshoppers are a part of nature. They were caused by the hot summer and the mild winter. Not by your wishing."

"Really?" Nellie asked.

"I'm sure of it," said Teacher. "It is not your fault." She patted Nellie's shoulder.

Relief poured through Nellie. She had told her worst secret, and everything was all right. Teacher still liked her. The grasshoppers were not Nellie's fault. Nellie pulled out her handkerchief—the one Teacher had given her during that recess many months ago. She wiped her eyes and blew her nose. She felt lighter, like a ribbon lifted on the breeze.

"I know it can be hard," Teacher said. "You are a pioneer girl, Nellie. It is a difficult life. You will often face hard choices, and you will need to be brave very often. But there are many wonderful things ahead of you, too. You'll see." She squeezed Nellie's shoulder and stood up. Willie came back inside, and Teacher went over to check his letters.

Nellie folded the handkerchief into small squares. She thought about hard choices and about being brave. She knew her father had made a hard choice with the coffee beans, and she also knew that he had made the wrong choice. Maybe there was a way for her to start being as brave and good as Teacher wanted her to be. She had an idea.

Late that night, after Nellie's parents were asleep, Nellie crept out of bed. She did not put on her shoes or stockings. She stepped on silent bare feet through the darkness of the bedroom and the parlor. She opened the store door and closed it quietly behind her.

In the store she lit a lantern and pulled down two empty sacks from the shelf where her father kept them. She went over to the barrel of coffee beans. It seemed larger than she had remembered. But she had made up her mind.

Nellie reached in and took a handful of beans. She rolled each one between her fingers and held it up to the flickering lantern light. If it was a dyed navy bean, she put it in one sack. If it was a real coffee bean, she put it in the other.

She did not want her father to get in trouble. She knew this was not something he would ever do in normal times. She knew mixing in the navy beans was wrong, and she knew that he knew it, too. The only way she could think of to fix it was by picking out every wrong bean one by one.

Soon her eyes started to hurt, but she kept going. The ache spread to her temples. The sack of navy beans slowly grew heavier and heavier. The sack of coffee beans filled up much faster. Nellie had to fetch more sacks for the coffee beans.

She was dropping three dyed beans into the navy bean sack when the back door of the store opened. Her father stood there in his night-shirt with another lantern. Nellie froze.

Mr. Oleson looked at her. He looked at the sacks. A whole minute passed. Nellie did not know what to say.

Mr. Oleson stepped into the store and closed the door silently behind him. He came over to Nellie and set the lantern down beside hers. Then he took a handful of beans and slowly began picking through them. Dyed beans into one sack. Coffee beans into the other.

He did not say a word. He did not have to. But after a moment he reached out and set one hand on Nellie's head. Nellie knew without words that he was telling her she had done the right thing.

They went through the entire barrel of beans together. The night wore on, and slowly the pink-and-gold dawn began to creep through the streets. The sun was almost all the way above the horizon when they finished the last few beans.

Mr. Oleson stood up and stretched. He helped Nellie to her feet. He took the sacks of real coffee beans and poured them all back into the barrel, and he put the navy bean sack behind the counter.

"Time for breakfast," he said. Then he and

Nellie went into the parlor together.

That was the last day of school. Nellie was so tired, she could hardly keep her eyes open. But she opened them wide when Teacher sat down next to her. Teacher was holding a thin green book. Gold letters were on the front, but they were drawn to look like vines were covering them.

"I found something you might like," Teacher said. "I've heard you talk about the city of New York many times. I know you would like to live there one day."

"Oh, yes!" Nellie said, her face lighting up. "I think it is the most beautiful city in the world."

"You're not the only one who thinks so," said Teacher. "Have you ever heard of a poet named Walt Whitman?"

Nellie shook her head. Teacher opened the book to a page where she had put a green ribbon marker.

"This is a poem he wrote called 'Mannahatta,'" Teacher said. "It is about how much he loves New York."

She read the poem out loud to Nellie. Nellie

didn't understand all the words, but she understood the feeling of the poem.

"*I was asking for something specific and perfect for my city,*"

Teacher read,

"*Whereupon lo! upsprang the aboriginal name!*"

She looked at Nellie. "He means the Indian word for New York City—Mannahatta," Teacher explained. Nellie nodded.

"*Now I see what there is in a name,*"

Teacher went on,

"*a word, liquid, sane, unruly, musical, self-sufficient,*
I see that the word of my city is that word from of old,
Because I see that word nested in nests of"

water-bays, superb,
Rich, hemm'd thick all around with
sailships and steamships, an island
sixteen miles long, solid-founded,
Numberless crowded streets, high growths
of iron, slender, strong, light, splendidly
uprising toward clear skies."

As the words poured out, like gold coins spilling over a white tablecloth, Nellie could feel her heart getting lighter. There was more, then finally:

"The summer air, the bright sun shining,
and the sailing clouds aloft,
The winter snows, the sleigh-bells, the
broken ice in the river, passing along up
or down with the flood-tide or ebb-tide,
The mechanics of the city, the masters,
well-form'd, beautiful-faced, looking
you straight in the eyes,
Trottoirs throng'd, vehicles, Broadway, the
women, the shops and shows,
A million people—manners free and

superb—open voices—hospitality—the
most courageous and friendly young men,
City of hurried and sparkling waters! city
of spires and masts!
City nested in bays! my city!"

Teacher closed the book. Nellie felt like her head was ringing with the most glorious words she had ever heard.

"If you liked that," Teacher said, smiling at Nellie's shining eyes, "you may copy it out for yourself. That can be your last assignment of the school year." She gave Nellie a piece of clean white writing paper and a pencil, and Nellie began to copy the poem in her neatest printing.

Splendidly uprising toward clear skies, Nellie wrote. She felt like she was splendidly uprising herself. She forgot about Laura Ingalls. She forgot about school yard games and the leeches trick. She forgot about the grasshopper plague and her parents' worries about money. They all went clear out of her head as she thought about New York. *The summer air, the bright sun shining, and the sailing clouds aloft.* She was only a little girl now, but one day she would be grown and she could do what she liked. Then she would go back to New York. She would be a lady and she would be happy, and all the sad things that had happened to her would only be stories from long ago.

City of hurried and sparkling waters! Nellie wrote. A smile spread over her face. *City nested in bays! my city!*